Martyr's Fire

· BOOK THREE ·
MERLIN'S IMMORTALS

Sigmund Brouwer

WATERBROOK
PRESS

Martyr's Fire
Published by WaterBrook Press
12265 Oracle Boulevard, Suite 200
Colorado Springs, Colorado 80921

The characters and events in this book are fictional, and any resemblance to actual persons or events is coincidental.

Trade Paperback ISBN 978-1-4000-7156-2
eBook ISBN 978-0-307-73209-5

Cover design by Mark Ford

Published in the United States by WaterBrook Multnomah, an imprint of the Crown Publishing Group, a division of Penguin Random House LLC, New York.

WaterBrook and its deer colophon are registered trademarks of Penguin Random House LLC.

Library of Congress Cataloging-in-Publication Data
Brouwer, Sigmund, 1959–
    Martyr's fire / Sigmund Brouwer.—First edition.
        pages cm.— (Merlin's immortals ; book 3)
    Merlin's immortals is a revised and expanded version of The winds of light series.
    ISBN 978-1-4000-7156-2 (pbk.)—ISBN 978-0-307-73209-5
    [1. Druids and druidism—Fiction. 2. Knights and knighthood—Fiction. 3. Civilization, Medieval—Fiction. 4. Christian life—Fiction. 5. Great Britain—History—Medieval period, 1066-1485—Fiction.] I. Title.
    PZ7.B79984Mat 2013
    [Fic]—dc23
                                                    2013019561

Printed in the United States of America
2015

10 9 8 7 6 5 4 3 2

SPRING, NORTHERN ENGLAND—AD 1313

The man that Isabelle faced was wealthy. And handsome, except for the stub where his left ear had been, now half-covered by hair. She could tell by the shift of his shoulders and the intensity of his gaze that he was enthralled by her, as indeed were nearly all men. Yet he was not Thomas. She spent hours dreaming that one day, Thomas, too, would be enthralled.

The man before her now had been on his horse, crossing a pasture that overlooked the town of York, clustered behind the high stone walls that protected it. With occasional clouds throwing brief shadows as they crossed overhead, she'd waited in sunshine, knowing that this was along his regular path to York from hunting in the moors. She'd been sitting on a blanket like a woman of leisure, dressed in fine silks, a basket beside her.

He was tall and slim, wearing the clothes of a nobleman. He'd dismounted and looked around, as if wondering where her servants might be. She had risen from the blanket and now lifted the basket with food.

"If you've been riding long," she purred, "you must be hungry. And I've been waiting for you."

She set the basket on the ground and leaned down to lift out a piece of thick buttered bread and pieces of rich cheese.

As she expected, he took it without hesitation. "You know who I am, then?"

"Of course," she answered.

He smiled with pride.

He was Michael of York, the son of the earl who had enlisted Thomas's army to prevail against the Scots not so long ago. As he tore off a chunk of bread and stuffed it into his mouth, he looked around again. Not with the eye of a man wary of a trap, but with the sharp glance of a predator. She was in front of him and so alone. And he was a rich and powerful man, accustomed to being offered what he wanted—or to taking it whether it was offered or not. Obvious on her neck was jewelry that was worth a year's wages for a working man. If he had the heart of a thief, and she knew he did, his mind would have been on her apparent helplessness.

Since no noblewoman should be alone in a field because the dangers were too great, the apparent helplessness should have made him suspicious. But men were fools.

"Mead?" she asked, holding up a chalice.

He took it without a word, as if he were entitled to it. He rammed some cheese into his mouth first, then washed it down with the honey wine.

"You've been waiting for me," Michael said, with a grin that came too close to a leer.

"With a message from those who watched you cut off your own ear."

His smile froze, just for an instant. Then he laughed.

"From anyone but a lady as lovely as yourself, I would take that accusation as an insult. And I would answer it accordingly."

"It is a dangerous accusation," she agreed. "If your father ever had proof that you severed your own ear to force him to attack Magnus, you would be thrown in prison and disinherited."

"You are very alone here." He gestured at the open pasture. "You would be wise not to anger me."

He placed his right hand on the hilt of his knife, hanging from a sheath on a gold-studded belt.

"And you would be wise to listen to me," she said. "After all, your father already questions your loyalty, does he not? After the trial by ordeal, did he not leave Magnus believing that Thomas is an ally and that you had deceived him?"

Michael's face pinched. He was beginning to suspect a trap. But his next words suggested that he believed the trap came from the earl.

"I will speak to you as I have repeatedly spoken to my father: I do not know the men who attacked me and cut off my ear. All I know is that I was given a message to deliver and told it was from Thomas. Obviously, those who cut off my ear were the ones deceitful about Thomas. Not me. Go back to my father and tell him this."

"Your father did not send me," she said. She tossed him a heavy ring. "Look closely at the symbol. Those of the symbol are the ones who sent me."

He caught it in his left hand and studied it. He glanced at her and closed his fist around the ring. He kept his right hand on the handle of his knife.

"I don't believe you." His words were certain enough, but not the tone.

"Let me repeat what you were told by those of the symbol. You were promised that if you delivered a letter to your father, along with your ear, pretending it was a letter from Thomas, that your father would go to war and take the castle of Magnus. And that Magnus would be yours."

Isabelle knew this was truth. She'd been hidden behind trees, watching the discussion, seeing greed cross this man's face as he calculated what small price it would cost for him to obtain a kingdom—his deception and his ear.

"Lies," he said, smiling.

"The man who made you that promise," she said, "was my father. Richard Mewburn, who ruled Magnus until Thomas took it from him."

She watched his smile fade as he thought through the implications. This was not something that a person could guess—proof to him that she knew for certain. And if she knew of that secret conversation, then she likely knew much more.

Michael lifted his hand away from his knife. "Please tell Lord Mewburn that I had no intention of harming you."

"Of course not," she said. "We are just having a conversation. So tell me. If my father were to deliver York to you, would you, in return, help him secure Magnus?"

"York cannot be mine while my father is the earl," he answered. It was an oblique answer. Nothing in it openly suggested disloyalty. Yet it was an invitation to continue.

"A man who is willing to cut off his own ear is a man hungry for power," Isabelle said. "This time, however, what we ask of you will be far less painful."

Michael's face reflected obvious relief before once again contorting into dismay. "But I was already promised that Magnus would fall. It did not. The trial by ordeal that Thomas faced and survived—"

"Nothing will be asked of you until Magnus falls," Isabelle said. "But believe me, it will. Very soon."

TWO

Each morning, the guards on the castle walls expected Tiny John to appear shortly after *tierce*, the ringing of the bells that marked the nine o'clock devotional services. By then, Tiny John would already have visited half the shopkeepers' stalls in Magnus.

The guards had good reason to watch for him; few were those who had not been relieved of loose coins by the rascal pickpocket. A temporary loss of silver—because Tiny John would return it without fail the next day—meant nothing. It was the ribbing of other guards that always left the victim red faced and huffing with indignation. After all, how could any military man keep self-respect if robbed by a boy?

None, however, were guards who could carry a grudge against Tiny John. He had been in Magnus since Thomas's arrival the previous summer. The lopsided grin that flashed from his smudged face was welcomed like the bright colors of a cheerful bird in every corner of the village, especially throughout an exhausting and long winter.

And, even without the charm of a born rascal, Tiny John was always safe within Magnus. The lord, Thomas, considered him a special—if untamable—friend, and that gave Tiny John immunity within the kingdom.

Before the bells of tierce stopped echoing in the spring morning air, Tiny John had already scampered from the first castle wall turret to the next. He dodged between the two gruff guards like a puppy whirling with glee among clumsy cattle.

"'Tis a fine kettle of fish, soldier Alfred!" Tiny John shouted through his grin at the second guard. "All the tongues in town waggle about the sly looks you earn from the tanner's daughter. And with her betrothed to a mason, at that!"

Tiny John waited, hunched over with his hands on his knees, ready for flight after the delivered provocation.

"Let me get a grasp a' you," soldier Alfred grunted as he lunged at Tiny John, "and then we'll see how eager you might be to discuss these matters."

Tiny John laughed, then ducked to his right. And made a rare mistake. He misjudged the slipperiness of the wet stone below his feet and fell flat backward.

"Ho! Ho!" A moment later, the soldier scooped him into burly arms, grabbed him by the scruff of his shirt and the back of his trousers, and hoisted his head and shoulders over the castle walls.

"Scoundrel," Alfred said, laughing, "tell me what you see below."

"Water." Tiny John gasped. A weak spring sun glinted gray off the waves of the small lake that surrounded the castle island.

"Water indeed. Perhaps you'll find that fine kettle of fish you mentioned?"

"Wonderful jest," Tiny John managed, though still obviously winded. "'Tis easy to understand why the tanner's daughter would be taken with a man such as yourself."

"Aargh!" Alfred grunted. "What's to be done with you?"

"A reward, perhaps?" Tiny John asked.

Alfred set him back down on his feet. "Reward indeed. Be on your way, and be glad I don't reward you with a cuff across the ears."

"I speak truth," Tiny John protested. "Because of me, you shall be the first to sound the alarm and, in return, be rewarded for your vigilance."

"Eh?" Alfred squinted as he followed Tiny John's pointing arm to look beyond the lake.

"There," Tiny John said firmly, "from the trees at the edge of the valley. A progression of fifteen men. None on horseback."

It took several minutes for Alfred to detect the faraway movement. Then he shouted for a messenger to reach the sheriff of Magnus.

Moments later, Alfred shouted again. This time in disgust at his now-empty pouch.

Tiny John, of course, had disappeared.

THREE

Rich, thick tapestries covered the walls of the royal chamber. Low benches lined each side, designed to give supplicants rest as they waited each morning for decisions from their lord.

Thomas leaned casually against the large ornate chair that served as his throne. He waited for the huge double doors at the front to close behind the man entering. His sheriff, Robert of Uleran.

Thomas's last glimpse beyond, as usual, was of the four guards posted out front, each armed with a long pike and short sword. And, as usual, it irritated him to be reminded that double guard duty remained necessary to protect his life, here in his own castle.

"The arrival of fifteen men?" Thomas asked to break their solitary silence.

"Exactly as Alfred spoke," Robert of Uleran replied to his lord. "Although I confess I am surprised by his accuracy and the earliness of his warning. He is not known for sharp eyes."

Thomas pulled one of the long padded benches away from the wall and sat down. With a motion of his hand, he invited Robert to do the same.

"Have the visitors been thoroughly searched?" Thomas asked.

Robert of Uleran froze his movement halfway to his seat and frowned at Thomas.

The mixture of hurt and surprise in Robert's wrinkled, battle-scarred face caused Thomas to chuckle soothingly. "Ho! You'd think I had just pulled a dagger!"

"You may as well have, m'lord," Robert of Uleran grumbled. "To even suggest my men might shirk their duty."

Thomas clapped the man on the shoulder. "My humblest apologies. Of course they have been searched. I grow accustomed to covering obvious ground in this chamber."

Mollified, the big man finally eased himself onto the bench. "We searched them thrice. There is something about their procession that disturbs me. Even if they do claim to be men of God."

Thomas raised an eyebrow.

Robert of Uleran nodded once. "They carry nothing except the usual travel bags, a cart with a large wrapped object, a sealed vial, and a message for the Lord of Magnus."

"Could the wrapped object be a weapon?"

Robert let out a breath. "That occurred to me too. But it seems more like a statue. I don't see how that might be considered a weapon."

"A vial?" Thomas repeated. "Any danger in that?"

"Only for the superstitious." Robert of Uleran scowled. "They claim it contains the blood of a martyr."

Thomas snorted. "Simply another religious spectacle, designed to draw yet more money from even the most poverty stricken. To which martyr does this supposed relic belong?"

The sheriff stood and paced briefly before spinning on his heels. He looked directly into the eyes of Thomas, lord of Magnus.

"Which martyr?" Robert of Uleran repeated softly. "'Tis said to be the blood of St. Thomas the Apostle. The Doubter."

Normal chaos reigned in the large hall opposite the royal chamber. The huge fire at the side of the hall crackled and hissed as fat dripped from the pig roasting on a spit above. Servants and maids scurried in all directions to prepare for the upcoming daily meal. Already, the table across the hall, high upon a platform, was set with pewter plates. Rough wooden tables running the entire length of the hall, still empty of any food, were crowded with people. Some rested as they waited to see Thomas, while others merely absorbed the liveliness of the hall. There were men armed with swords, bows, and large wolfhounds; women both in fine dress and in rags.

Standing to the side of all this activity, aloof to the world, were fifteen men garbed in simple brown robes. They did not bother to look up when the doors opened. When summoned by Robert of Uleran, two of the men broke away from the group. Thomas crossed his arms beneath his purple cloak and awaited their approach.

He said nothing as his guards closed the doors, leaving the four of them alone in the chamber.

The silence hung heavy. Thomas made it no secret that he was inspecting them, although their loose clothing hid much. Thomas could not tell if they were soft and fat, or hardened athletes. He could only be certain that they were large men, both of them.

The first, who stared back at Thomas with black eyes of flint, had a broad, unlined forehead and a blond beard, cropped short. His nostrils flared slightly with each breath, an unconscious betrayal of heightened awareness.

The second appeared slightly older, perhaps because his skin above and under his scraggly beard was etched with pockmarks. His eyes were flat and unreadable.

Tight skin gleamed at the tops of the men's skulls, suggesting a very recent shave.

Thomas fought a shiver. Something about their unblinking acceptance of his impertinent appraisal suggested arrogance, like the smugness of a cat, indifferent to the struggling mouse trapped within its paws.

Thomas set his features as cold as the North Sea only thirty miles to the east. And waited. Sarah's wisdom was never far from his mind. She alone had prepared him to rule Magnus, and thus far, her teachings had not failed him.

Finally, the younger of the two monks coughed.

It was the sign of weakness for which Thomas had been taught to wait. "You wished an audience," Thomas said.

"We come from afar, from—," the younger man began.

Thomas held up his hand and slowly and coldly stressed each word. "You wished an audience." Normally, he was not this arrogant. Normally, he wasn't concerned about protocol and appearing to be the ruling authority just below the level of a king. But something about the fifteen men suggested a small army, and he didn't want to show the slightest hesitation in bringing to bear his entire power.

The older man coughed this time. "M'lord, we beg that you might grant us a brief moment to present our request."

Thomas turned his back on the men to show his lack of concern, knowing Robert would let nothing befall him as walked to his throne. He took his time settling into the seat and heaved a sigh before speaking. "Granted. You may make your introductions."

Something about this felt like the moments just before battle.

"I am Hugh de Gainfort," the dark-haired man said, attempting to take a step closer, only to be stopped short by Robert's tree trunk–like arm.

"Lord Thomas can hear you fine from there, my good man," Robert said patronizingly.

Hugh reddened slightly but continued as though nothing unexpected had occurred. "And my fellow clergyman is Edmund of Byrne."

Thomas leaned forward and steepled his fingers in thought below his chin.

"Clergymen?" he said. "You appear to be neither Franciscan nor Cistercian monks. And representatives of Rome already serve Magnus."

Hugh shook his head. "We are from the true church. We are the Priests of the Holy Grail."

"Priests, I presume, in search of the Holy Grail."

Hugh's next words chilled Thomas. "No. We guard the Holy Grail."

Robert of Uleran's laugh rang through the stone chamber. "Ho! And I suppose we're to believe you guard King Arthur's sword in the stone as well!"

For a moment, Hugh's eyes widened.

Yet the moment passed so quickly that Thomas immediately doubted he had seen any reaction.

"The Grail and King Arthur's sword have much in common," Hugh replied with scorn. "And only fools believe that the passing of centuries can wash away the truth."

Robert of Uleran opened his mouth and drew a breath. Thomas held up his hand again to silence any argument.

"Your procession brings a saint's relic," Thomas said, ignoring Hugh's outburst to reestablish authority. "Have you come to squeeze profit from my people with the blood of St. Thomas? Or have you requested audience to siphon directly from the treasury of Magnus?"

Edmund clucked as if Thomas were a naughty child. "Those who leech blood from the poor shall be punished soon enough for their methods. No, we are here to preach the truth."

"Yes," Hugh continued. "Our only duty is to deliver our message to whomever hungers for it. We have coin for our lodging in Magnus, so we beg no charity. Instead, we simply request that you allow us to speak freely among your people during our stay."

"How long do you plan to grace my land with your...truth?"

"As long as they will have us." Something in Hugh's tone caused the hairs on Thomas's neck to stand.

"If the people are not fooled?" Thomas asked.

"Are you, too, a doubting Thomas?"

Thomas rose to signal the audience was over. "And if permission is refused?"

Hugh bowed in a mocking gesture.

"Let us put aside these games of power, shall we, young man? We both know that your villagers have heard rumors of the martyr's blood and the miracle to come. You dare not refuse now." The priest's voice became silky with deadliness. "For if you do, our miracles will become your curses."

FOUR

The Priests of the Holy Grail waited until the middle of the afternoon on their second day to demonstrate their first miracle.

The low, gray clouds of the previous week had been broken by a sun so strong that it almost felt like summer. To the villagers of Magnus, it was a good omen. These priests, it seemed, had banished the dismal spring chill.

Now the streets were hectic with activity. Men, women, and children were anxious to be out of doors and in the bright sunshine. Shopkeepers shouted good-natured abuses at one another across the rapidly drying mud streets. Housewives joyfully bartered down to the last farthing so as to enjoy the heat of the sun on their shoulders for a bit longer. Servants shook bedding free of winter's fleas and dirt. Dogs lay sprawled at the sides of buildings, the promise of summer leaving them too lazy to nose among the scrap heaps.

The Priests of the Holy Grail were quick to take advantage of the joviality.

There were only five now, speaking at the corner of the church building that dominated the center of Magnus. The others rested quietly in nearby shadows. They took turns in shifts, constantly calling out and delivering selected sermons, answering questions, and warding off insults from the less believing.

Hugh de Gainfort was leading this group of five into the hours of the early afternoon. His brown robe made him swelter in the heat; that much was obvious by the beads of oily sweat that dotted his shaven skull.

Still, he spoke with power, certainty, and charisma. It was not unusual for twenty or thirty villagers to be gathered at any given moment.

He looked beyond the crowd, into the shadows of the church, then nodded so slightly that any observer would have doubted the action had been made.

"Miracles shall prove we are the bearers of God's truth." Hugh raised his voice without interrupting his sentence as he completed that slight nod. "And as we promised upon our arrival, one shall now appear!"

The crowd buzzed with murmurs.

"Yes!" Hugh shouted. "Draw forward, believers and unbelievers of Magnus! Before the *none* bells chime, you shall witness the signs of a new age of truth!"

Hugh swept his arms in a circle. "Go," he urged the crowd. "Go now and return with friends and family! Bring back with you all those to be saved! For what you see will be a sure sign of blessing!"

The other four priests, all garbed in brown and with skulls shaven, began chanting. "The promised miracle shall deliver blessings to all who witness. The promised miracle shall deliver blessings to all who witness."

For several seconds, no one in the crowd reacted.

Hugh roared, "Go forth into Magnus! Return immediately, but do not return alone! Go!"

An old man hobbled away. Then a woman with a small child and swaddled infant. Finally, the rest of the crowd turned, almost in unison, and spread in all directions. Some ran. Some stumbled as they looked back at Hugh, as though afraid he might perform the miracle in their absence.

Almost immediately, Edmund of Byrne left the shadows. He carried a statue nearly half his height and set it down carefully in front of Hugh.

"Well spoken, my good man." He patted the top of the statue. "Remember: wait until they are nearly frenzied; then deliver. It is the only way to be sure that Thomas of Magnus will suffer the same fate as the once-proud Earl of York."

Edmund smiled savagely as he finished speaking. "After all, is there not a certain sweetness in casting a man into his own dungeon?"

⚜

A great, noisy crowd had filled the small square in front of the stone church. The promise of unexpected entertainment broke life's monotony and struggle.

Hugh de Gainfort raised his arms and silence fell. Beneath bright sun, his pockmarks became pebbled shadows across the skin of his face.

"People of Magnus!" he called. "Many of you doubt the Priests of the Holy Grail. Some of you have ridiculed us since our arrival two days ago. Because we are kind and compassionate, we forgive your insults, delivered in ignorance. But know this: After you witness the miracle of the Madonna, such insults will not be forgiven. After today, none of you will be excused for not following our truth!"

Excited and angry murmurings issued from the crowd.

Hugh lifted the statue and, with seemingly little effort, held it aloft.

"Behold, the Madonna, the statue of the sainted Mother Mary!"

The noise stopped instantly. All in the crowd strained for a better view.

The sun-whitened statue was of a woman with her head slightly bowed beneath a veil. A long flowing cape covered most of her body. Only her feet, clad in sandals, and her hands, folded in prayer, appeared from beneath the cape.

Few, though, ever remembered the details of folded hands or sandaled feet. The Madonna's face captivated all who looked, such were the carved details of exquisite agony. The Madonna's eyes were even more haunting than the pain etched so clearly in the plaster face. Those eyes were deep crystal, a luminous blue that seemed to search the hearts of every person in the crowd.

"Mother Mary knew well of the Holy Grail," Hugh said in deep, slow words as he set the statue down again. "She blessed this statue for our own priests, thirteen centuries ago. Our own priests, who already held the sacred Holy Grail. Thus, she established us as the one true church!"

A voice from the entrance to the church interrupted Hugh. "This is not a story to be believed! This is blasphemy against the holy pope and the church of Rome!"

Hugh turned slowly to face his challenger.

The thin man at the church entrance wore a loose black robe. His face was pale with anger, his fists clenched at his sides.

"Ah!" Hugh proclaimed loudly for his large audience. "A representative of the oppressors of the people!"

This shift startled the priest. "Oppressors?"

"Oppressors!" Hugh's voice gained in resonance, as if he were a trained actor. "You have set the rules according to a religion of convenience! A religion designed to give priests and kings control over the people!"

The priest stood on his toes in rage. "This…is…vile!" he said in a strained scream. "Someone call the Lord of Magnus!"

One of Hugh's men slipped through the crowd and placed a hand on the priest's shoulder and squeezed the priest into silence.

No one else moved.

Hugh's smile did not reach his cold black eyes. "The truth shall speak for itself," Hugh said gravely. He turned back to the people. "Shall we put truth to the test?"

"Yes!" came the shout. "Truth to the test!"

The priest's eyes widened like a trapped animal's. Hugh could see the fear that drained the priest's face of color. In total, there were fifteen large men, and who knew what arms they carried beneath their cloaks? Obviously, the priest was in no position to defy such a large crowd.

Hugh held up his arms again. Immediate silence followed.

"What say you?" Hugh queried the priest without deigning to glance back. "Or do you fear of the results?"

More long silence. Finally the priest croaked, "I have no fear."

Hugh smiled at the crowd in front of him. He noted their flushed faces, their concentration on his words.

"This Madonna," he said with a theatrical flourish, "blessed by the Mother Mary herself, shall tell us the truth. Let us take her inside the church. If the priest speaks truth, the Madonna will remain as she is. However, if falseness against God resides within, the Madonna will weep in sadness!"

Even as Hugh finished speaking, those at the back of the crowd began to push forward. Excited babble washed over all of them. None wanted to miss the test.

"And," he thundered, "when the truth is revealed, the new and faithful followers of the Priests of the Holy Grail will soon be led to the Grail itself!"

At this, not even Hugh's upraised arms could stop the avalanche of shouting. The legendary Grail promised blessings to all who touched it!

Hugh took the statue into his arms and turned to face the church. He marched forward.

Without pausing to acknowledge the priest, he walked through the deep shadows of the church's entrance and into the quiet coolness beyond, until he reached the altar at the front. He cleared the lit candles and set the statue down, making sure it faced the gathered people.

Soon the church was full. Every eye strained to see the Madonna's face. Every throat was dry with expectation.

"Dear Mother Mary," Hugh cried to the curved ceiling above, "is this a house worthy of your presence?"

The statue, of course, remained mute. So skillful, however, was Hugh's performance that some in the audience leaned forward as if expecting a reply.

Hugh fell to his knees and clasped his hands and begged at the statue's feet.

"Dear Mother Mary," Hugh cried again, "is this a house worthy of your presence?"

For a dozen heartbeats, he stayed on his knees, silent, head bowed, hands clasped high above him. Then he looked upward at the statue, and moaned.

He stood in triumph and pointed.

"Behold," he shouted, "the Madonna weeps!"

Three elderly women in the front rows fainted. Grown men crossed themselves. Children shrieked in terror. And all stared in horror and fascination at the statue.

Even in the dimly filtered light at the front of the church, water visibly glistened in the Madonna's eyes. As each second passed, another large drop broke from each eye and slowly rolled downward.

FIVE

Thomas made it his custom to greet each dawn from the eastern ramparts of the castle walls. At that hour, the wind had yet to rise on the moors. Often, mist rose from the lake that surrounded Magnus, and behind Thomas, the town would lay silent as he lost himself in thought and absorbed the beauty of the sun's rays breaking over the tops of the faraway hills to cut sharp shadows into the dips and swells of the land.

There, on the ramparts in the quiet of a new day, Thomas found great solace in silence that was a near prayer. It was here, and not in the rituals intoned by priests who insisted they alone could mediate between God and man, that he felt closest to accepting that a loving Creator had fashioned this world. There were moments he could almost hear a call to open his heart, to accept this, to believe that God listened to each man and woman who called upon His name.

Even in those moments, which seemed to him like the natural hesitation that a deer might show as it surveyed open and dangerous ground that sloped to a stream of pure waters, he could not overcome his suspicion.

Thomas well knew three classes comprised society: those who work, the peasants; those who fought, the nobility; and those who pray, the clergy.

Since praying was easier than work and safer than fighting, a life in the church was an attractive career. Because of this, many abused their positions of power. Like the monks who abused him as a boy, leaders in the church were as prone to glut themselves off plates of gold and silver as the nobles.

The hard-earned money of their peasant charges bought jewels and rings, fine horses, and expensive hounds and hawks.

It was not difficult to claim shelter in the wings of the Roman church. A test for clerical status was simple: because literacy and education were so rare, any man who could read—or memorize and recite, as was more often the case—a Latin text from the Bible could claim "benefit of clergy." This was especially valuable if one had committed a crime. Common thieves to cold-blooded murderers were given complete exemption from the courts of the land and tried instead by the church. And, since the laws within the church forbade mutilation or death, and since it was too expensive for the church to maintain its own prisons, it relied on spiritual penalties as punishment. At the very worst, a cleric might face a fine or a light whipping.

Thus, Thomas lived in uneasy alliance with the church in Magnus. No matter how powerful the ruler, the power of the church was equal. More dreaded by an earl or king than a sieging army was the threat of excommunication. After all, if the people believed that a ruler's power was given directly by God, how could that ruler maintain power if the church made him an outcast? Though he had been coolly accepted by the priest of Magnus, Thomas still felt outcast in his own kingdom. Each morning and each night, when Thomas found himself alone with his thoughts, the questions that haunted him rose to the surface of his consciousness, in empty hopes that they might one day be answered.

The old man who once cast the sun into darkness and directed me here from the gallows where a knight was about to die, falsely accused—who was he and how did he know of my secret dream and duty to conquer Magnus?

William, the valiant and scarred knight who befriended me and helped me win the castle that once belonged to his own lord, departed suddenly and without explanation. Why? Where could he have gone?

The foul candle maker, Geoffrey, and Isabelle, the beautiful and treacherous daughter of the vanquished Lord Mewburn, were both found to be Druid spies. I captured and imprisoned Geoffrey in the dungeons of Magnus, and yet he escaped. How?

The midnight messenger, Katherine: she spent all those years in Magnus disguised beneath bandages as a scarred freak. Was she, too, a false sorcerer, seeking to win Magnus from me? Or was she truly my friend, now banished unfairly, by my command, from this kingdom?

What is the secret of Magnus?

The early rays of sun that warmed Thomas on the eastern ramparts had never replied to these silent questions.

On this day, less than a week after the arrival of the Priests of the Holy Grail, Thomas now had other urgent problems to occupy him as he walked the ramparts.

Not even the enthusiastic puppy that had helped Thomas discover Katherine's and Isabelle's deceptions during the siege on Magnus was enough of a distraction during these terrible days.

Thomas reached down and scratched the puppy's dark head. "Haven't I fed you enough in repayment for your services? Surely you have better things to do than spend hours of your day searching for me."

In the previous months, Thomas had asked for Robert of Uleran's help with an experiment. Robert would take the puppy anywhere in Magnus and release it, and then Thomas would go on his way. The pup would reappear, sometimes in minutes, sometimes in a few hours, sometimes the next day. Robert found it amusing; Thomas found it perplexing. He had not asked for the dog's loyalty and in fact was even reluctant to give it a name.

Still, he had to admit, he'd been growing fond of the animal's presence and persistence, even as he wondered if that was a sign of weakness. And weakness was not something he dared show. Ever. To anyone, save one man.

A man with a calming and gentle wisdom. It took no time at all for Thomas to decide that this day required a visit to this man.

⚜

"Five days of nonsense about the Holy Grail!" exploded Thomas. "A statue that weeps. And the blood of a martyr that clots and unclots as directed by prayer! I am at my wit's end, Gervaise. It is almost enough for me to sympathize with the priests of Rome."

Gervaise knelt in the rich dirt of the church's garden, weeding with peaceful precision. "Then the matter must be grave." The elderly man chuckled without looking up from his task. "Brave would be the man to gamble that you ever side with Rome."

Thomas paced two steps past Gervaise on the stone path that meandered through the garden, then whirled and paced back. "Jest if you will, but do not be surprised if you find yourself without gainful work when the priest you serve is cast from this very church."

Gervaise hummed in the sunshine beating down upon his stooped shoulders. His gray hair was combed straight back, as usual, and showed no sign of sweat. His voice was deep and rich in tone, and matched in strength the lines of humor and character etched in his face. He had thick, gnarled fingers, as capable of threading the most delicate of needles as of clawing among the roots of the roughest bush, which he did now with great patience.

Among wide, low shrubs stood carefully pruned bushes, almost ready to bloom. The greatest treasure for Gervaise among these were his roses. Each summer, he would coax forth petals of white, of pink, of yellow. All were considered prizes of delight by the noblewomen of Magnus.

Gervaise gently loosened another weed from the roots of a rosebush. He placed the weed atop a rapidly drying pile an arm's length away. "The sun proves itself to be quite hot these days," he said in a leisurely tone. "It does wonders for these precious plants. Unfortunately, it also encourages the weeds."

Thomas sighed. "Gervaise, do you not understand what happens here? With these ridiculous miracles, the Priests of the Holy Grail have practically wooed the entire population of Magnus."

Gervaise straightened with effort, then finally turned to regard the young master of Magnus.

"I understand it is much too late to prevent what surely must happen next. The horse has escaped the stable, Thomas. Therefore, I will not worry about closing the gate." Gervaise swept his arms in a broad motion to indicate the garden. "So I shall direct my efforts where they will have effect."

Thomas stopped halfway through another stride. "So you agree with me about the dangers," he accused. "And what do you believe will happen next?"

"The Priests of the Holy Grail will replace those within the church now," Gervaise said mildly. "Then, I suspect, from the pulpit they will preach sedition."

"Sedition?" Thomas exploded again. "Impossible. To set their hand against the church is one thing, but to rebel against the royal order is yet another!"

Gervaise wiped the dirt from his knees and walked to a bench half-hidden by overhanging branches.

Thomas followed.

"Impossible?" Gervaise echoed softly as he sat. "Last summer you conquered Magnus and delivered all of us from the oppression of our former master. Yet how have you spent your winter? Relaxed and unafraid?"

Thomas sat alongside the old man. He did not answer immediately.

Around them, the spring birds joyfully caroled, oblivious to the pressing matters of state at hand.

"You know the opposite," Thomas said slowly, knowing where his answer would lead. "Day after day, each meal, each glass of wine tested first for poison by giving tiny amounts to mice. Each visitor searched thoroughly for daggers or other hidden weapons before an audience with me. Double guards posted at the door to my bedchamber each night. Guards at the entrance to this garden, ready to protect me at the slightest alarm. I am a prisoner within my own castle."

"Thus," Gervaise said, with no trace of triumph, "you are no stranger to rebellion. Why, then, do you persist in thinking it may not come from another source?"

"Yet these are priests against priests, Holy Grail against those from Rome, each seeking authority in religious matters, not matters of state," Thomas countered.

Gervaise shook his head and pursed his lips in a frown. "Thomas, these new priests carry powerful weapons! The weeping Madonna. The blood of St. Thomas. And the promise of the Holy Grail."

Gervaise paused, then added, "Thomas, tell me: Should the Priests of the Holy Grail become your enemy, how would you fight them?"

Thomas opened his mouth to retort, then slowly shut it as he realized the implications.

"Yes," Gervaise said, "pray these men do not seek your power, for they cannot be fought by sword. Every man, woman, and child within Magnus would turn against you."

Six

Thomas leaned on the ledge near the window and waited until Robert of Uleran had entered and closed the door to the bedchamber.

"Attack, my beast!" Thomas called out. "Attack!"

With a high-pitched yipping, the puppy bolted from beneath a bench and flung himself with enthusiasm at Robert's ankle.

"Spare me, m'lord!" cried Robert of Uleran in fake terror. "Spare me from this savage monster!"

The puppy had a firm grip of the leather upper of Robert's boot, and no shaking could free him.

Thomas laughed so hard he could barely speak. "Tickle him behind the ears, good Robert. He's an easy one to fool."

Robert of Uleran reached down, then stopped and glared at Thomas with suspicion. "He'll not piddle on my boot instead?"

"You guessed my secret weapon," Thomas hooted.

"Bah." Robert reached down, soothed the puppy with soft words and a gentle touch, then scooped him up and quickly dropped him into Thomas's arms.

"Go on," Robert said to the puppy. "Now discharge your royal duties. Then we'll see who has the last laugh."

"Rich jest," Thomas said, cradling the dog in the crook of his right arm. He rubbed the top of the puppy's head thoughtfully. "Would that all of Magnus could be tamed this easily."

Robert of Uleran nodded, then spoke above the panting of the puppy.

"You seem far from ill, m'lord. The reports had led me to believe I would find you half-dead beneath the covers of your bed."

Thomas smiled but sobered quickly. "Do not let the rumor rest. It serves our purpose for all to believe the fever grips me so badly that I cannot leave this room."

"M'lord?"

"Robert, three days ago—with the miracle of the weeping statue—the Priests of the Holy Grail won the mantle of authority in the church of Magnus. They preach now openly from the pulpit, and the former priest has been banished. It is not a good sign."

"It cannot be bad," Robert protested. "Let the religious orders fight among themselves."

"I wish I could agree," Thomas said. The puppy chewed on the end of his sleeve and sighed with satisfaction. "But I must be sure there is no threat to the rest of Magnus."

Robert raised his eyebrows in a silent question.

"All winter," Thomas continued, "we have been hidden in these towers, away from the people. Aside from the servants in this keep and those who request audience, I have seen no one. I have almost been a prisoner."

"The Druids, m'lord," Robert of Uleran said in a whisper. "You cannot be blamed for precautions."

"Perhaps not. But now I have little idea what concerns these people in everyday life. I hear their legal problems in the throne room, but little else."

"But—"

"How do they feel about these new priests?" Thomas interrupted. "Someone must go among them and discover this."

Robert of Uleran straightened. "I will send someone immediately."

"A guard?" Thomas asked. "A knight? Do you believe such a man will receive the confidence of housewives and beggars?"

Robert of Uleran slowly shook his head.

"I thought you might agree. Therefore, someone must spend a day on the streets, perhaps disguised as a beggar."

"But who, m'lord? It must be someone we trust. And I am too large and well known for such a task."

"Who do I trust better than myself?" Thomas countered.

"You could send Tiny John," Robert said.

"Yes, I thought of that. But he is known for his loyalty to me. Anyone speaking to him knows it will be like speaking directly to me. So again, I'll simply be told what people believe I want to be told."

Robert scratched his beard thoughtfully. "I can think of no one, m'lord."

Thomas smiled brightly. "Good, then we are in agreement."

Robert frowned. "M'lord?"

"I shall have to do it. Let us waste no time in preparing my disguise."

SEVEN

T homas felt a degree of freedom that surprised him.

Gone was the long purple cape he wore publicly as lord of Magnus. Gone were the soft linen underclothing, the rings, and the sword and scabbard that went with his position.

In their stead were coarse, dirty rags for clothing, no jewelry, and—as Thomas had copied from his long-departed knight friend—a short sword ingeniously hidden in a sheath strapped between his shoulder blades. To pull the sword free, Thomas would only have to reach as if scratching his back.

With Robert of Uleran's help, Thomas had dyed his skin several shades darker with the juice of boiled bark. This, he hoped, would give him the rough texture and appearance of a person who spent too much time outside in the bitter cold wind or the baking sun.

Thomas had cut his hair short in ragged patches and scraped dark grease repeatedly with his hands to impact the filth beneath his fingernails. He planned to spend at least two days among the peasants of Magnus, and only the blindest of fools would fail to notice clean hands on a street beggar.

But how should he disguise his features?

Robert of Uleran had suggested an eye patch. Many in the land were disfigured or crippled, and many of those by necessity were forced to beg or die. True, it was not common, yet it was not remarkable for a beggar with one eye to appear among the poor.

Thus disguised, Thomas let his shoulders sag and added a limp as he slipped unnoticed through the great banquet hall among the crowds of morning visitors.

As he forced his way through the dizzying noise, smells, and sights, he felt a degree of shame for how quickly he'd begun to believe that he was above all those in the shadows of his castle.

"Step aside, scum!" bellowed a large man guiding a mule loaded with leather. When Thomas did not react fast enough for the man's taste, he was shoved back into a crowd of people on the side of the street.

"Watch yourself!" another shouted at Thomas. Hands grasped and pulled at him, while other hands pushed him away in disgust. One well-placed kick to the back of his knee pitched Thomas forward, and when he stood upright again, he knew he'd no longer need to fake his limp.

Thomas moved ahead, handicapped by the lack of depth of vision forced upon him by using only one eye.

Still, he refused to be downcast. He'd entered Magnus as a penniless orphan and had felt no shame for it. In fact, the experience served as a reminder that he needed to be true to himself, not to what the trappings of lordship gave him.

The scene, of course, looked identical to his first time in Magnus. Shops crowded the streets so tightly that the more crooked of the buildings actually leaned into neighboring roofs. Space among the people who bustled in front of him was equally difficult to find.

Thomas did not let his renewed sightseeing stop him from carefully placing each limped footstep. Avoiding the mess of emptied chamber pots and the waste of sheep, calf, or pig innards thrown out by the butchers demanded one's full attention.

Pigs squealed, donkeys brayed in protest against heavy carts, and dogs barked, all a backdrop of noise against the hum of people busy in the sunshine.

Thomas sighed and turned backward to squint against that sunshine as he gazed at the large keep of Magnus that dominated the center of the village. If he didn't return, would it matter? What if he walked away, lived as a fighting man, and traveled across the land? Magnus would continue to exist. People would continue living as if he'd never been.

He had enough silver to travel. To confirm that, Thomas reached for his hidden pouch containing two silver coins. Beggar or not, he did not relish going hungry in the eve or on the morrow—

Thomas groaned.

Only five minutes away from the castle and he had been picked as clean as a country fool by those grasping hands in the crowd.

EIGHT

T is our good fortune the weather holds," the old woman cackled to Thomas. "Or the night would promise us much worse than empty bellies. The roof leaks horribly in any rain at all!"

Thomas grunted.

The old woman chose to accept his grunt as one of agreement. She moved herself closer to Thomas and snuggled against his side in the straw.

Which was worse—the cloying barnyard smell of the dirty stable straw, or the stale, unwashed odor of the old woman who sought him for warmth? His skin prickled; already he could feel, or imagine he felt, the fleas transferring from the old woman to him. The piece of fat he wore around his neck in a tiny cage to lure the biting bugs would be covered in no time.

Besides, Thomas did not know if he agreed with her or not. It had been so long since he had felt hunger he thought he might have preferred a rainy, cold night for the sake of being fed.

He stared into the darkness around him. Vague shapes moved; those horses, at least, were content.

The old woman burped, releasing a sour gas that did little to improve the immediate situation.

"I wonder," he asked, "why there are not more of us seeking shelter here in the stables. Do others fear the soldiers of Magnus?"

Thomas, however, knew well they did not. As lord, he had commanded his men not to harry the poor who commonly used the stables as a last resort. So why were they empty?

The old woman snorted. "The others choose the church as sanctuary."

"Ah," Thomas said. He maintained his role as a wandering beggar, freshly arrived in Magnus. "I had heard the priest of Magnus would give food and a roof to any who pledged work the following day."

Thomas smiled quickly to himself as he finished his words. After all, he and Gervaise had set that policy themselves, to allow the penniless their pride and to stop the abuse of charity by the lazy.

Much to his surprise, the old woman laughed cruelly. "No longer! Have you not heard? That priest has been replaced by the men of the Holy Grail."

"Indeed?" Thomas asked.

"Indeed. They brought miracles with them—a weeping statue, if you can believe it, boy! The people of Magnus fell all over themselves to see it and the blood of St. Thomas the Apostle. The Priests of the Holy Grail banished the former priest from his very own church!"

"I understand little, then," Thomas admitted. "You say the former priest is not in the church. Where, then, do the less fortunate stay each night, if not here in the stables or at the church?"

The old woman shifted, heedless of the elbow that forced a gasp from Thomas.

"I did not say the church was empty," she told him. "Only that the poor need not pledge a day's services in exchange for food and lodging. Instead, the Priests of the Holy Grail demand an oath of loyalty."

"What!" Thomas bolted upright and bumped the woman solidly. He almost forgot himself in his outrage. He forced himself to relax again.

"Lad," the old woman admonished, "give warning the next time. My old bones cannot take such movement."

"I beg pardon," Thomas said, much more quietly. "It seems such a strange requirement, pledging an oath." He fought to keep his voice curious instead of angry. "I had thought that an oath of loyalty could only be pledged to those who rule."

The old woman cackled again. "Are you so fresh from the countryside that your good eye and both your ears are still plugged with manure? These priests have promised the Holy Grail to those who follow. With such power, how could they not soon rule?"

Once again, Thomas fought frustration at the invincibility of his opponents. When he felt he could speak calmly again, he pretended little interest.

"What do you know of this Grail?" he asked casually. "And its power therein?"

The old woman clutched Thomas tighter as the evening chill settled upon them.

"Had you no parents, lad? No one to instruct you in common legends?"

She reacted instantly to his sudden stillness.

"It is my turn to beg pardon," she said softly. "There are too many orphans in the land."

"'Tis nothing." Thomas waved a hand in the darkness, as if brushing away memories.

She patted his chest as if to soothe him before speaking again. "The Holy Grail," she repeated. "A story to pass the time of any night."

Her voice became oddly beautiful as it dropped into a storytelling chant. As Thomas listened, the stable around him seemed far away. He no longer sucked the air carefully between his teeth to lessen the stench. The straw no longer stabbed him with tiny pinpricks. And the burden of the woman leaning against him lessened. Thomas let himself be carried away by her voice, back through lost centuries to the Round Table of King Arthur's court.

"Long ago," she said softly, "at Camelot, there was a fellowship of knights so noble…"

The Holy Grail, she told Thomas, was the cup that Christ had used at the Last Supper, the night before He was to be crucified. This cup was later obtained by a wealthy Jew, Joseph of Arimathaea, who undertook to care for Christ's body before burial. When Christ's body disappeared after the third day in the tomb, Joseph was accused of stealing it and was thrown into prison and deprived of food.

"It was in that prison cell that Christ Himself appeared in a blaze of light and entrusted the cup to Joseph's care! It was then that Christ instructed Joseph in the mystery of the Lord's Supper and in certain other secrets! It is these secrets that make the Holy Grail so powerful!"

"These secrets?" Thomas interrupted.

"No one knows," she admitted. "But it matters little. How can these secrets not help but be marvelous?"

Only because people want them to be marvelous, Thomas thought.

She told him the rest of the legend in awed tones, as if whispered words in the black of the stable might reach those priests of power.

Joseph was miraculously kept alive by a dove that entered his cell every day and deposited a wafer into the cup. After he was released, he was joined by his sister and her husband and a small group of followers. They traveled overseas into exile, careful to guard the cup on their journey, and formed the First Table of the Holy Grail.

"This table was meant to represent the Table of the Last Supper," the old woman said with reverence. "One seat was always empty, the seat of Judas, the betrayer. A member of the company once tried sitting there and was swallowed up!"

Thomas marveled at the woman's unwavering superstitious belief.

"Go on," he said gently. "This takes place long before King Arthur, does it not?"

"Oh yes," she said quickly. "Joseph of Arimathaea sailed here to our great island and set up both the first Christian church at Glastonbury and, somewhere nearby, the Grail Castle."

She sighed. "Alas, in time the Grail Keeper lost his faith, and the entire land around the castle became barren and known as the Waste Land, and strangely, could not be reached by travelers. The land—and the Grail— remained lost for many generations."

The woman settled deeper against him. Her silence continued for so long that Thomas suspected she had fallen asleep.

"Until King Arthur?" he prompted.

"No need to hurry me," she said crossly. "I had closed my eyes to see in my mind those noble knights of yesteryear. Too few are pleasant thoughts for an old, forgotten woman."

Then, as if remembering the impatience of youth, she patted Thomas's arm in forgiveness. "Yes, lad. Until King Arthur. At the Round Table, the Holy Grail appeared once, floating in a beam of sunlight. Those great knights pledged themselves to go in search of it."

Thomas settled back for a long story. Many were the escapades of King Arthur and his men, many the adventures in search of the Holy Grail, and many were the hours passed by people in its telling and retelling.

Thomas heard again of the perilous tests faced by Sir Lancelot, and his son, Sir Galahad, and Sir Bors, Sir Percival, and the others. Thomas heard again how Sir Percival, after wandering for five years in the wilderness, found the Holy Grail and healed the Grail Keeper, making the Waste Land once again flower. Thomas heard again how Percival, Galahad, and Bors continued their journey until reaching a holy city in the East, where they learned the mysterious secrets of the Grail and saw it taken into heaven.

She told it well, this legend that captured all imaginations. But she did not finish where the legend usually ended.

"And now," she said, "these priests offer to us the blood of a martyr of ancient times, blood that clots, then unclots after their prayer. They offer us the weeping statue of the Mother Mary. And they speak intimately of the Holy Grail, returned rightfully to them, with its powers to be shared among their followers!"

Thomas felt his chest grow tight. Indeed, these were the rumors he had feared. "These followers," he said cautiously, "what must they do to receive the benefits of the Holy Grail?"

The old woman clucked. "The same as the poor must do to receive shelter. Pledge an oath of loyalty, one that surpasses loyalty to the Lord of Magnus, or any other earthly lord."

These were the rumors that had not yet reached him, the rumors he had sought by leaving his castle keep. How much time, upon his return, did he have left to combat these priests?

Another thought struck Thomas.

"Yet you are here," Thomas said into the darkness to the woman curled against his side. "Here in the stable and not at the church. Why have you not pledged loyalty to this great power for the benefits of food and lodging?"

The old woman sighed. "An oath of loyalty is not to be pledged lightly. And many years ago, when I had beauty and dreams, I pledged mine to the former lord of Magnus."

"Y-yet"—Thomas stammered suddenly at her impossible words—"was that not the lord who oppressed Magnus so cruelly, the one whom Lord Thomas so recently overcame?"

"You know much for a wandering beggar," she said sharply. "Especially for one ignorant of the Holy Grail."

"I have heard much in my first day here," Thomas countered quickly.

"So be it," the old woman agreed, then continued. "I did not swear an oath to that tyrant. No, my pledge of loyalty was given to the lord who reigned twenty years earlier, a kinder lord who lost Magnus to the tyrant Lord Mewburn."

Thomas marveled. This woman showed great loyalty to the same lord Thomas had avenged by reconquering Magnus. *Yes,* Thomas thought, *I will reward this old woman later, when I leave off this disguise and resume the duties of the lord of Magnus.*

He was given no time to ponder further.

The nearby horses stamped nervously at a sudden rustling at the entrance to the stable.

"Hide beneath the straw!" the old woman hissed. "We'll not be found!"

She began to burrow.

While Thomas did not share her fear, he wanted to maintain his role as a half-blind beggar, and a half-blind beggar in a strange town would do as she instructed. So he burrowed with her until they were nearly covered.

Many moments passed. Strangely, a small whimpering reached them.

Straw poked in Thomas's ears and his closed, uncovered eye. Despite his curiosity, he held himself perfectly still.

Somehow, a patter of light footsteps approached their hiding spot directly and with no hesitation. From nowhere, a cold, wet object bumped against his nose, and Thomas nearly yelped with surprise. Then a warm tongue found his face, and Thomas recognized the intruder was nothing more alarming than a friendly puppy. Thomas could not help the name that leaped into his mind.

Yes, it was Beast.

Beast wriggled with joy and whined as he pushed up against Thomas.

"Thomas?" a voice called.

Tiny John! What meaning did this hold?

Thomas sat up and shook the straw free from his clothes. He held Beast away from him so that the licking would cease.

"I am here," Thomas said from beneath the straw. He ignored the surprised flinch of the old woman. "What urgent business brings you in pursuit?"

"I followed the puppy," Tiny John explained. "And he found you exactly as Robert predicted in his last words to me."

Thomas stood quickly and with a cold lump of fear in his stomach.

"His last words? What has occurred?"

Tiny John's voice trembled. "The castle has fallen without a fight, m'lord. Few were those who dared resist the Priests of the Holy Grail."

"That...cannot...be," Thomas uttered. His knees felt weak.

"I recognize you!" the old woman cried as she stood beside Thomas.

"The deception could not be helped," Thomas muttered as his mind tried to grasp the impossible.

The old woman clouted Thomas. "Not you, ragamuffin! The boy. Dark as it is, I know his voice. Tiny John. He is a friend of the Lord of Magnus! And a friend to the poor. Why, more than once he has raided the banquet hall and brought us sweetmeats and flagons of wine. The boy could pick a bird clean of its feathers and not wake it from its perch. Why, he..."

The old woman's voice quavered. "Wait. What deception? You spoke of deception?" Then a quiet gasp of comprehension. "The boy called you Thomas! Not our Thomas? Lord of Magnus?"

"Aye, indeed. I am Thomas." He pulled of his eye patch and flung it into the straw. "And by Tiny John's account, now the former lord of Magnus."

The old woman groaned and sat heavily.

"M'lord," Tiny John blurted, "the priests appeared within the castle as if from the very walls! Like hordes of rats. They—"

"Robert of Uleran," Thomas interrupted with a leaden voice. He wanted to sit beside the old woman and, along with her, moan in low tones. "How did he die?"

"Die?"

"You informed me that he spoke his last words."

"Last words to me, m'lord. Guards were falling in all directions, slapping themselves as they fell! The priests claimed it was the hand of God and called for all to lay down their arms. It was then that Robert of Uleran pushed this puppy into my arms and told me to flee, told me to give you warning so that you'd not return to the castle."

Thomas shifted Beast into the crook of his left arm and gripped Tiny John's shoulder fiercely with his right hand. "You know not the fate of Robert of Uleran?"

"No, m'lord. There was great confusion. I'm sorry."

Thomas relaxed his grip. "You needn't apologize, John. You did right by finding me. Now we just have to hope that no one else does."

NINE

The shadows of the castle spires had hardly darkened with the rising sun, yet already the news was old.

Magnus has fallen to the Priests of the Holy Grail!

Some rejoiced, almost in religious ecstasy. After all, there had been the miracles of the weeping statue and the blood of the martyr! And now, stories of how the guards had fallen without a fight! Surely the Grail must appear next!

Others were saddened. Wisely they did not show this emotion, for who could guess the intentions of Magnus's new masters? Yet they grieved for the loss of Thomas, who, they were told, had mysteriously vanished as the castle fell to the priests. These mourners knew that Thomas had ruled with compassion and intelligence. They were still grateful to Thomas for releasing them from bondage to a cruel lord less than a year before.

And few, although too many, were those whose eyes glinted with greed to hear that Thomas had been disposed, or that the Priests of the Holy Grail had offered a brick of the purest gold to the man who might capture him.

Thomas limped along the edge of the streets. It took little effort to add that limp to his step; yesterday's brutal kick was this day's growing bruise, and a sleepless, chilled night had stiffened his leg considerably. He'd put his eye patch on again, meager protection though it was.

Beneath his rags, he carried the puppy in the crook of his left arm.

There was comfort in the warm softness of the animal against his skin. Occasionally, Beast would lick Thomas's arm, a solace that never failed to elicit a small smile, despite his troubles.

The smile did not reach anyone, however. Thomas kept his gaze lowered on each halting step along the street. Whispers of the massive bounty placed upon his head had reached his ears. *If the wrong pair of sharp eyes recognizes me despite the rags and eye patch…if the old woman does not keep her vow of secrecy…if Tiny John is captured by bounty hunters…*

Yet Thomas could not remain hidden, cowed in a dark shadow somewhere within Magnus. If he were to survive, he must escape the castle island. To escape, he needed help from the one person he trusted and hoped was still alive.

And to reach that person, he must enter the lions' den. So Thomas shuffled and limped to the edge of the church building and prayed no Holy Grail priest would inquire too closely about the business of a starving beggar.

At the rear of the stone building, Thomas followed the same garden path he had walked—was it only two days before?—so proudly in his purple cape as lord of Magnus.

He rounded a bend of the path and saw the familiar figure of Gervaise, kneeling in the soil, pulling weeds with methodical delicacy. Thomas almost straightened and cried aloud in relief, but something stopped him.

What was this strangeness?

Not weeds piled in neat bundles beside Gervaise, but the rosebushes, roots already wilting in the sun. The most precious plants in the garden! Why would Gervaise root them out so diligently?

Thomas sucked in his breath. Was this a message?

It disturbed Thomas so much that, instead of a joyful call, he continued to limp slowly toward the old man.

"Good sir," Thomas croaked, "alms for the poor? I've not eaten in two days."

Gervaise yanked another rosebush free from the soil and did not look up.

"Gervaise," Thomas hissed, "it is I!"

The old man laid the bush on the nearest bundle and shuffled sideways on his knees to an unworked patch of soil.

"Of course it is you, Thomas. And not a moment too soon," Gervaise grumbled without looking up. "Removing these roses has robbed me of five years of toil. This price counts little, however, for you noticed and took it as warning."

Gervaise paused, then said, "Ask your question again, as if I were deaf. And add insult to your words. We must appear strangers to each other."

Thomas hesitated a moment, then raised his voice. "Are you deaf, you old cur? I've not eaten in two days."

"Do as the other beggars," Gervaise instructed loudly with acted impatience. "Enter the church and pledge allegiance to the Priests of the Holy Grail."

Thomas stopped abruptly as Gervaise turned his head to look upward in response.

The mangled right side of the old man's face was swollen purple. Lines of dried blood showed the trails of cruel, deep slashes. His right eye was swelled shut, and his nose was bent and pushed sideways at an angle that made Thomas gag.

"The Priests of the Grail know you and I are friends," Gervaise said calmly, without moving his head. "This was done to encourage me to deliver you into their hands. And as you may have guessed, they observe me now from the church windows and from the trees behind you."

Thomas blinked back tears.

"If you do not go into the church shortly," Gervaise continued in a low voice, "those watchers will suspect you and hunt you down. They may be within hearing distance. Ask me now which priest to see. Do not forget the insults."

Thomas hoped his voice would not choke as he forced the words into a scornful snarl. "Worthless donkey! Instruct me well the priest to seek, ere I add to the scars on your face!"

"Enter the church without hesitation," Gervaise commanded quietly. "You must reach the altar. Then—" Gervaise looked past Thomas, then back at Thomas. Gervaise bowed his head as if afraid.

But his voice continued strong but low. "Thomas, the panel beneath the side of the altar that holds the candles—kick it sharply near the bottom. Twice. It will open. Use the passage for escape."

"But—"

Gervaise then looked Thomas squarely in the eyes. Exhaustion and strain marked the other side of the old man's face. "After sixty steps, you must make the leap of faith. Understand? Make the leap of faith. You will find the knowledge you need near the burning water."

Thomas began to shake his head. "Burning water? What kind of madness do you—"

"You must reach the altar. If they suspect who you are, Magnus and all its history is lost."

"Gervaise...," Thomas pleaded.

Gervaise sighed and turned toward his digging. "If I speak more to you, they will surely suspect. Walk away."

Thomas shifted his balance.

Thomas then limped onward, toward the entrance of the church.

He kept his head low as tears rolled from his eyes.

TEN

At the wide doors to the church, Thomas discovered some of his fears had been unfounded. Instead of being a lone and highly noticeable figure, he was only one of many entering the building.

Once inside, he stopped to let his swimming eyes adjust to the sudden dimness.

Gervaise, Thomas sorrowed, *what evil has forced itself upon us?*

Men and women stood in a long line down the center of the nave, the main chamber of the church. At the front of the church, in the chancel that held the altar, stood a priest who briefly dipped his hands in a vessel from a stand near the altar, then touched the forehead of the person bowed below his hands.

"Move on, man!" a fat man growled at Thomas from behind. "This is no place to daydream. Not with blessings to be had."

Thomas told himself he could not spare any thoughts of grief, only thoughts of action. He fell in behind two women and slowly limped toward the front of the church.

The measured pace of the line gave Thomas time to look around the structure he'd seen so many times before. This time, however, he looked with the anxious eyes of stalked prey. Vaulted stone ceilings gave an air of majesty and magnified the slightest noise, so that all inside only spoke in careful whispers. The nave where Thomas stood was, of course, clear of any objects except support pillars. While rumors had reached Magnus that London churches contained long bench seats called pews for the worshipers, no person bothered believing such nonsense. People had always stood to worship, and that was the natural order of the Lord's Day.

There were at least four Priests of the Holy Grail posted throughout the church—one at the front and three on the sides of the nave. Thomas tried to study their movements without betraying obvious interest.

Was it fear, or did he imagine they in turn studied him?

Thomas also wondered at his own lunacy. How much trust should he have placed in Gervaise? Had the blows to the old man's head addled him? What could exist beneath the altar? And how would the altar be reached—and kicked—without the notice of the four Priests of the Holy Grail?

Yet Thomas moved forward. He had no choice. Those behind him pressed heavily.

And even if I could turn away, what good would it do? There was no place to hide in Magnus, and if he bolted now, surely the watchers would then decide he had been more than a cruel-hearted beggar sent inside by Gervaise to seek alms.

His heart pounded harder and harder as step by step the line advanced to the priest at the front.

Closer now, Thomas recognized him as Hugh de Gainfort. The priest, garbed in royal purple robes, dipped his hand in the liquid.

"Partake of the water of the symbol of the Grail," the scar-faced man intoned, "and henceforth be loyal to the Grail itself, and to its bearers. Blessings will be sure to follow. Amen."

The woman kissed his hand.

The line moved ahead.

The next person moved up.

Hugh spoke the same words.

Would the puppy in Thomas's arms remain quiet? Or would he draw unwanted attention?

"Partake of the water of the symbol of the Grail..."

Thomas wondered if the priest would hear the thumping of his heart long before he reached the front. Only ten people stood between him and Hugh de Gainfort, and Thomas could see no way to reach the altar beyond without drawing attention.

What trouble had Gervaise cast him into?

"...and henceforth be loyal to the Grail itself, and to its bearers. Blessings will be sure to follow. Amen."

The light of the sun through the reds and blues of the stained-glass windows cast soft shadows upon Hugh de Gainfort, so that if Thomas did not look closely, he did not see hatred glittering in those eyes—the same hatred Thomas had felt during their brief audience earlier in the castle keep.

Would he be recognized during the blessing? If not, how could he reach the altar unseen? What truth could there be in the old man's instructions? And even if the passage revealed itself, how could he enter unnoticed?

Thomas swallowed in an effort to moisten his suddenly dry throat. This was madness, and he was only one step away from a blessing that...

It was his turn.

"Partake of the water of the symbol of the Grail"—de Gainfort's hand dipped into the water, and wet fingers brushed against Thomas's forehead— "and henceforth be loyal to the Grail itself, and to its bearers. Blessings will be sure to follow. Amen."

Thomas started to turn away. The movement drew Hugh's eyes briefly. Suddenly those black eyes widened.

"It is you!" the priest hissed. He opened his mouth to shout.

Thomas reacted with a move Robert of Uleran had taught him—a move he had practiced hundreds of times but had never been forced to use. He twisted his shoulders away from the priest, then spun back to drive forward his right hand in a shortened swing. In that blink of an eye, Thomas managed to hit his target with his clenched fist, middle knuckle slightly protruding. The point of the knuckle found its target, a small bone between the ribs, just above the priest's stomach.

The air left the priest's lungs with an audible *pop*. He clutched himself and began to sway, wind knocked out thoroughly.

It happened so quickly that those behind Thomas were not sure what they had seen.

Before Thomas could decide how best to flee, a terrifying crash overpowered the cacophony of whispers. One of the arched windows fell inward, burying a nearby priest. White light from sudden sun flooded the church and danced off rising dust.

Hugh de Gainfort dropped to his knees, still winded so badly he could barely breathe, let alone draw enough air to shout.

Then another crash as the window farther down tumbled inward.

It could only be Gervaise!

Thomas did not hesitate. Whatever sacrifice the old man had just made to create the diversion must not be wasted.

Thomas darted to the altar.

What had the old man said? The panel beneath the candles was to be kicked sharply near the bottom. Twice.

Thomas glanced to see if Hugh de Gainfort had seen him, but the priest had sagged into a limp bundle. All others stared in frozen horror at the destruction. If a passage truly existed, Thomas might escape without witnesses.

Thomas kicked once. Twice.

Soundlessly, the panel swung inward, revealing a black square beneath the altar wide enough to fit a large man. A spring hinge ensured that it would snap shut.

Then a scream from outside the building. What price was Gervaise paying to buy Thomas these extra moments?

Thomas bit his lower lip. The old man's sacrifice should not be made in vain. Thomas ignored the pain in his leg and sat quickly, so that his feet dangled over the edge. He pulled Beast from beneath his arm.

"Gervaise, my friend, if you go to your death, so do I."

Thomas put both arms around the puppy to shield him, then let himself drop into the darkness.

ELEVEN

D eath arrived for neither.

Thomas dropped through the air for half a heartbeat. He closed his eyes and braced for the crush of impact, splattering him against the black unknown.

Then, incredibly, it felt as if arms began to wrap him tightly. A great resistance began to slow his fall.

Those arms grew tighter, then brushed against his face. In the same moment, Thomas felt growing friction against his body and realized these were not the arms of a savior, but a giant cloth sleeve, tapered into an ever-narrowing tube.

It slowed him almost to a standstill as the tube grew so tight that the fabric squeezed against his face.

Then, just as it seemed he had more to fear from suffocation than from splintered bones and shredded flesh, his feet popped into open air, and he slid loose from his cloth prison.

Even though the final drop was less than the height of a chair, Thomas was not able to see the ground in time to absorb the impact; the jarring of his heels against hard ground forced loose a grunt of pain.

He recovered his breath quickly and strained to see around him.

"Wherever we are, Beast," Thomas said, "we can assume it is a better alternative to what was in store for us above."

Thomas was glad in this darkness for the company of his furry friend. Except for his own voice and the whimpers of the puppy, there was silence.

It told Thomas that the Priests of the Holy Grail had not seen him escape. They did not know, then, of the passage beneath the altar.

He felt his heart begin to slow. Without immediate pursuit, he could move slowly and thoughtfully.

Thomas reached around him to explore for walls. In the darkness, he could not even see the movement of his own arm. He pulled his eye patch loose. It did not help his vision.

"What is this place?" Thomas asked, then forced himself to smile. "Ah, Beast, you do not answer. That is a good sign. For if I were mad or dreaming, you would speak."

The puppy whined at the gentle sadness in his master's tone and squirmed in Thomas's arms. He offered comfort with well-placed licks.

"Enough!" Thomas said through a laugh. "Next, you'll try to soothe me by wetting yourself!"

He set the puppy down but felt a wave of panic when Beast snuffled away from his leg. He had no idea if the ground gave way to holes or rifts. He or the puppy could break a leg. Yet what could he do but explore?

Thomas sobered immediately.

So much had happened so quickly. Only yesterday, he had ruled the island castle of Magnus, and by extension, the kingdom around it. Today he was a fugitive, marked for death or worse by the offer of a brick of gold for his head. Because of him, his friends had suffered equally.

Robert of Uleran's fate was unknown.

Gervaise might have paid the ultimate price for his sacrifice of distraction.

Tiny John could only wander the streets and hope the Priests of the Holy Grail would not place any importance on his freedom.

And now?

Thomas took a deep breath to steady his nerves.

Now he was in pitch blackness, somewhere below Magnus in a pit or passage he had never known existed.

To return to Magnus, even if possible, endangered his life. Yet how long could he remain, blind, within the bowels of the earth?

A new thought struck Thomas with such force that he sucked air in sharply.

Gervaise knew.

Gervaise knew of the trapdoor below the altar.

More thoughts tumbled through Thomas's cluttered mind.

Warnings of evil within Magnus. Whispered secrets that had plagued him since first conquering the kingdom.

Surely this must be part of the mystery of Magnus. Yet if Gervaise knew, why had he not revealed it much earlier, before the arrival of the Priests of the Holy Grail? Thomas strained to remember the old man's words. *"After sixty steps, you must make the leap of faith. Understand? Make the leap of faith. You will find the knowledge you need near the burning water."*

Somewhere in this darkness, he would find the answer.

TWELVE

Despite darkness so deep that even a quarter hour of adjustment had failed to show the faintest light to his eyes, Thomas spoke in a conversational manner, as if he and the puppy were in bright sunshine, sharing the warmth of the spring day outside. "Well, Beast, he was right about the altar panel and provided for our escape. But what am I to make of this 'leap of faith' Gervaise has instructed me to make?"

The puppy whined in response.

"I would ask him if he were here, silly dog! Knowing Gervaise, he'd probably say something such as, 'Thomas, faith is difficult to explain,'" he said, imitating Gervaise's deep, calm voice. "'But with it, prayer eases the mind much.' How do I know He listens? That I cannot explain either."

A light patting reached Thomas as the puppy's tail thumped the ground to reflect contentment. Then a yip.

"Well, that's just the way he talks. Gervaise is not known for addressing the situation in front of you. He's a more subtle man." The puppy remained pressed against his feet. Thomas tucked his chin into his chest and mimicked the old man's voice. "You have a mind, Thomas. How can you remain so unwilling to learn? Just because some men have twisted this religion for their own purposes is no reason to cast away faith. Because the monks in your boyhood abbey showed such little faith is no reason to apply their falseness to the essential truth."

Thomas squatted and scratched the puppy's head. He reverted to his own voice and spoke almost absently, because his mind was already on the problems ahead. "As much as I do not want to believe, puppy, I cannot deny that twice I faced death, and twice I cried to the God in whom I did not want to believe. Explain that. We are here now because false priests seek to obscure the truth. And we must apply that to our situation—the darkness is obscuring our path. We cannot rely upon our eyes now, just as the people should not trust what they see performed by the Priests of the Holy Grail. We can only rely upon that which we know to be true, and in our case, that is Gervaise. And, as always, he speaks to me about a leap of faith."

Instead of answering, the puppy shifted his weight and settled for a nap.

"Not so soon," Thomas warned his small friend. "We can't let this time go to waste. He no doubt pays a great price for our freedom." Thomas shook off the memory of Gervaise's scream outside the church above. What had happened to the old man? Was he still alive? Nothing would come from worrying. Better to honor the man and his sacrifice by following his instructions.

"Our journey begins."

Thomas took his first halting step with courage, the result of three things: the calm from realizing the priests above did not know where he had vanished, the promise of an explanation when he found the burning water, and, strangely, from the puppy blundering into his legs each step he took. A companion, no matter his size, made the eerie silence easier to bear.

Thomas took his next step into a rough stone wall. His groping hand prevented any injury to his face, yet Thomas recoiled as if he had been struck. Any sudden contact, gentle or not, created awesome fear in this pitch-dark place.

Thomas pushed himself away, then thought again, and brought his right shoulder up to the wall.

"I'll feel my way along," he told the puppy, simply as a way to break the tension that brought sweat in rivers down his face despite the damp chill. "It will give me warning of twists and turns."

Thus, his fingers became his eyes.

Thomas patted the wall as he followed it, grimacing at real or imagined cobwebs. He stubbed his fingertips raw against outcrops of stone and stumbled occasionally against objects on the ground. Twice he patted empty air—as much a fright as the original contact against stone, and each time discovered another turn in the passage. He counted each step, remembering the strange message about a leap of faith. The puppy stayed with Thomas and did not complain.

Upon his sixtieth step, Thomas paused. There was nothing to indicate a leap of faith. What had the old man meant?

Two steps later, Thomas reached for the stone wall ahead of him and found nothing.

"Another turn," he muttered to the puppy. "This cannot be what the old man meant. Then why not warn me of the previous two? The shock of many more will kill me more surely than those priests."

He slowly began to pivot right, when a low, angry noise froze him.

It took a moment, but Thomas identified the echoes as growls of the puppy at his feet.

Thomas relaxed.

"Hush," he spoke downward, then moved to take his step.

The puppy growled again, with enough intensity to make the skin ripple down Thomas's back.

"Easy, my friend." Thomas knelt to soothe the puppy. The growling stopped.

Thomas stood and moved again. This time the puppy bit Thomas in the foot and growled louder.

"Whelp! Have you gone crazy?"

Thomas reached down to slap the puppy for his insolence, but couldn't find him in the dark.

He groped farther, patting the ground. First behind him, then to his side, then—

Ahead! The ground ahead had disappeared.

Thomas forgot the puppy. He patted the wall on his right, found the edge of the corner and slid his hand downward, finally kneeling to reach as low as possible. Where the corner met the ground, it was no longer a corner, but a surface that continued downward below the level of his feet.

The skin on his neck now prickled in fear.

"Beast," he cried softly. A whimper answered him.

Thomas, on his knees in his blindness in the dark, crawled backward two more paces, then eased himself onto his stomach.

Feeling safer on his belly, Thomas inched forward again, feeling for the edge of the drop-off with his extended right hand. When he reached it, he kept his hand on the edge, but shuffled to his left, determined to find the width of the unseen chasm.

Seconds later, he found it, joined to the left wall.

Thomas was too spent with the jolts of fear to react with much more than a moan of despair.

"How deep?" he asked the puppy. "How far ahead to the other side?"

Thomas crawled ahead as far as he dare. With his dangling hand, he reached down into the blackness. *After all, perhaps this drop is a mere foot or two,* he thought. *I could be stuck here forever, afraid to step downward.*

His exploring hand had found nothing. Even after drawing his sword and extending it to reach farther, he could not prove to himself that the drop was only a shallow ditch.

Long minutes later, he raised his head from the ground again. He knew he had three choices. Leap ahead and trust the chasm was narrow enough to cross. Drop into the chasm and trust its bottom was just beyond his reach. Or retrace his steps.

Thomas called the puppy closer and tried to find his ears in the darkness. The puppy found his hand first and gently licked as though cleaning his master. Thomas suddenly realized the puppy was licking away blood from his damaged fingers. He'd been so tense he'd not noticed when his skin went from raw to broken.

How could he possibly overcome this barrier?

Thomas shouted and listened for an echo. Would that tell him anything? Not enough to make any kind of decision about how deep or wide the chasm was.

A tiny flicker caught his eye.

Thomas almost missed it, so much had he given up on using vision to aid his senses.

He blinked, then squinted.

Five minutes passed.

Another minute. There! The flicker again. It brightened, then dropped to nothing. Thomas strained to focus and pinpoint its location. Ten agonizing minutes later, another flare, hardly more than a candle's last waver before being suddenly snuffed.

It dawned slowly upon Thomas.

A flame.

Burning water?

THIRTEEN

He was seeing the light of a far-off flame, light that flared rarely and softly. Light that reflected and bounced off the passageway across the chasm.

Thomas raised himself and sat, knees huddled against his chest. The puppy leaned against him, whining occasionally, growling for no apparent reason in other moments.

A phrase echoed through his head. *"Make the leap of faith."*

Why had the old man been so urgent with those five words? Why had he repeated those words and no other part of his instructions?

"Make the leap of faith."

It reminded him of part of a conversation he'd once held with Gervaise. To pass time, Thomas spoke aloud to the puppy.

"During the quiet of an early morning," Thomas said, "Gervaise told me this: 'No matter how much you learn or debate the existence of God, no matter how much you apply your mind to Him, you cannot satisfy your soul with a decision based on proof.'"

The puppy rested his chin on Thomas's upper thigh.

"The old man said there must come a time at the beginning of your faith when you let go and simply trust, a time when you make the leap of faith, something much like a…" Thomas faltered as he suddenly realized the significance of Gervaise's repeated words.

He finished the thought silently. *"Something much like a leap into the darkness."*

The conversation flooded Thomas's mind. They had talked often, usually in the early hours after Thomas had walked the ramparts of Magnus. This conversation had taken place barely a month after Thomas had conquered Magnus. Gervaise had talked simply of faith in answer to all of Thomas's questions.

"It is a leap into the darkness, Thomas," he had said. *"God awaits you on the other side. First your heart finds Him; then your mind will understand Him more clearly so that all evidence points toward the unshakable conclusion you could not find before, and after that leap, your faith will grow stronger with time. But faith, any faith, is trust and that small leap into darkness."*

"No, Gervaise," Thomas said aloud. "I cannot do this. You ask too much."

"After sixty steps, you must make the leap of faith. Understand? Make the leap of faith."

Yet how could Thomas blindly jump ahead? What lay on the other side? What lay below?

An encouraging thought struck him.

Magnus was surrounded by lake waters. Indeed, the wells of Magnus did not have to be dug deep before reaching water. And this passage was already below the surface. How far down, then, before reaching water from this passageway?

Might he drop his sword to test the depth of the chasm?

"Make the leap of faith."

No, he could not venture weaponless.

Might he drop Beast ahead to test the depth of the chasm? Or cast the Beast ahead to test the width?

"Make the leap of faith."

No. He knew that, while his brain compelled him to explore every option, his heart would not let him callously do something like this to the puppy. Not to an innocent creature. Not when Beast trusted him so.

"Make the leap of faith."

Thomas frowned. Had he not regarded Gervaise with equal trust? And if Thomas now showed such concern for the puppy, would not Gervaise show that much more concern for Thomas?

"Make the leap of faith."

Thomas finally allowed himself to decide what he had known since recalling the old man's words about faith.

He must leap into the darkness.

Ten times Thomas paced large steps backward from the edge of the chasm. Ten times he repaced them forward again, careful to reach down and ahead with his sword on the eighth, ninth, and tenth steps to establish he had not yet reached the edge.

"Beast," he said as he retraced his steps backward yet again, "if leap we must, I shall not do it from a standstill. Faith or not, I doubt Gervaise would encourage stupidity."

Thomas had debated briefly whether to leave the puppy behind. But only briefly. The extra weight was slight, and he could not bear to make it across safely and hear the abandoned whimpers of a puppy left for death.

Thomas squatted and felt for the line he had gouged into the ground to mark the ten paces away from the edge.

He rehearsed the planned action in his mind. He would sprint only eight steps—for he could not trust running paces to be as small as his ten carefully stretched and marked paces. On the eighth step, he would leap and dive and release the puppy. His hands would give him first warning of impact—how he hoped for that impact!—and at best he might knock loose his breath. The puppy would travel slightly farther, and at best tumble and roll.

At worst, neither would reach the other side of that unknown chasm in this terrible blackness.

Thomas drew a deep breath. He hugged the puppy once, then tucked him into the crook of his right arm.

"Make the leap of faith."

Thomas plunged ahead.

FOURTEEN

At full sprint, Thomas dove upward on the eighth step and left the ground.

In the black around him, he had no way to measure the height he reached, no way to measure how far forward he flew, and no way to measure how much he dropped.

It seemed to take forever, the rush of air in his ears, the half sob of fear escaping his throat, and the squirm of the puppy in his outstretched hands.

The puppy!

In midair, Thomas pushed him ahead and released him from his hands. Before he could even think of praying for his safety, or the safety of the puppy, the heels of his hands hit solid ground, and he bumped and skidded onto his nose and chin, then, as his head bounced upward, his chest and stomach.

Time, with him, skidded back to normal, and Thomas could count his heartbeats thudding in his ears.

Was he across? Or at the bottom of a shallow ditch?

The puppy's confused whimper sounded nearby.

Thomas coughed and rolled to his feet.

"My friend," he said, "we seem to be alive. But across?"

Thomas answered his own question by turning around and crawling back. Moments later, his hands found an edge!

Thomas grinned in the darkness.

The next eighty-eight steps took nearly an hour. Although the occasional flare of reflected light grew stronger and stronger, it provided little illumination, and Thomas dared not to risk another unseen chasm.

Finally, the flame itself!

As Thomas walked closer, the rising and falling light provided him more clues about the passage.

The walls were shored with large, square blocks of stone, unevenly placed. He understood immediately why his groping fingers had received such punishment in the total darkness behind him.

The passage was hardly higher than his head and wide enough to fit three men walking abreast.

Other than that, nothing. No clues as to the builders. No clues as to its reason for existence. No clues as to its age.

Thomas ran the final few steps to the light. The leg ache he had managed to forget in the previous few hours flared again with the extra movement, but he did not mind.

Gervaise had promised the knowledge he needed. It could only mean a message. And if Gervaise had managed to leave the message, Gervaise had managed to get out again. There was hope in that.

Thomas noted the source of the light. It was imbedded in the wall, as if a hand had scooped away part of the stone. A wick of cloth rose above a clear liquid, and from it came the solitary tongue of flame.

Burning water!

He did not examine the light long, because the puppy whined and sniffed at a leather sack barely visible in the shadows along the wall below the flame. Thomas pulled the sack away before the puppy could bury his nose in it entirely.

He understood the puppy's anxiousness as soon as he opened it.

Cheese. Bread. And cooked chicken legs. All wrapped in clean cloth.

Thank you, Gervaise. Sudden moisture filled Thomas's mouth as he realized how hungry he was. With his teeth, he ripped into a fat chicken leg, chewed a mouthful, then tore pieces free with his fingers to drop to the puppy.

More objects remained in the bag.

Thomas pulled free a large candle. He dipped the end into the flame in the wall and immediately doubled his light. Next from the bag came a candle holder, hooded so the bearer could walk and shed light without fear of killing the flame.

Finally, Thomas pulled free a rolled parchment, tied shut with a delicate ribbon.

He wiped chicken grease from his hands, then placed the candle holder on the ground and sat beside it.

The puppy nosed his palms for more food.

"Later," Thomas said absently. His fingers, no longer bleeding and suddenly without pain as he focused on the parchment, trembled as he pulled the ribbon loose and unrolled the scroll.

The inked letter was bold and well spaced, as if the writer had guessed Thomas might be forced to read it in dim light.

Thomas, if you read this, it is only because, as I feared, the
Druids, guised as Priests of the Holy Grail, have imprisoned you
in your own dungeon. Yet if you read this, it is because you dared
make the leap of faith I requested, and in so doing have proved
you are not a Druid.

Druids! The shock was as an arrow piercing his heart. Thomas rubbed his forehead in puzzlement. "Imprisoned in my own dungeon—I did not arrive here from the dungeon. And to suggest I might be a Druid—how could Gervaise even dare to think such a thing? I have spent the entire winter in fear of their return!"

Yes, my friend, the chasm you crossed was a test. Were you one of the Druids, you would have known that these passages and halls—

"Passages and halls?" Thomas sighed. This message created more mystery than it solved.

—are buried so deep in the island that anything more than several feet below their level would fill with water. You, as a Druid, would already be familiar with this. You, as a Druid, would have confidently stepped down and walked across, even without light to guide you. That you are reading this means you are not a Druid, for in that shallow, dry moat, I have placed a dozen adders.

Adders! Snakes with venom so potent that only a scratch of their poison could kill. A dozen adders! In the darkness, the puppy had not growled at the drop-off, but at what his nose had warned him of.

Thomas scratched the puppy behind the ears and shuddered at what might have happened had Gervaise not urged him to make the leap of faith.

Thus you now have my trust, Thomas. I regret I could not give it earlier. There is much to tell you, my friend, and I fear by the time you return to Magnus, I will not be alive to be the one who reveals to you the epic struggle between the Druids and the Immortals who were established by Merlin himself.

Merlin! Mention again of the ancient days of King Arthur. For Merlin, King Arthur's advisor, had become as much a legend as the king himself!

I cannot say much in this letter, for who is to guess what others may stumble across it, should you not take the leap of faith to be the first to arrive here. Let me simply ask you to consider the books of your childhood. It was not chance that they were placed near you, those books of ancient knowledge from faraway lands. It was not chance that one of us was there to raise you, to teach you, to guide you, to urge you to reconquer Magnus, to show you the way. It was not chance that I spread the legend of the delivering angel shortly before your birth.

These new words were not the piercing of an arrow, but now the bludgeoning of a club. Gervaise knew of those precious books hidden near the abbey? At the significance of the message, Thomas could hardly breathe. He remembered the night he had conquered Magnus on the wings of an angel, how the entire population of Magnus had gathered enough strength from his arrival to overthrow its evil lord, simply because of a legend all believed. This had been planned before he was born?

Yet none of this knowledge I could share, Thomas, much as I treasured our conversations. For many years passed with you alone in the abbey. We did not know if they had discovered you and converted you. We did not know if you were one of them, allowed to conquer in appearance only so that we might reveal the final secrets of Magnus to you, secrets so important I cannot even hint of them now.

To arrive here, you trusted me. I beg of you to continue that
trust. Your destiny has grown even more crucial—we did not
expect the Druids to act so boldly, so soon. Even now, perhaps
they have the power to conquer completely. You, as a born Im-
mortal, must stop them.

"A born Immortal. I am a born Immortal? Gervaise, how can you reveal so much, yet reveal so little?" Thomas protested aloud.

Follow this passage, Thomas. It will take you to safety. Return
to your books and search for the answers in them. Ask yourself:
Where is the source? Trust no one. The stakes are too high. The
Druids must not prevail.

FIFTEEN

R ecount for me, my daughter, how events have unfolded since our arrival here in York." Lord Mewburn spoke to Isabelle in his usual commanding tone. "Tell me how I ensured the earl would be imprisoned."

The two of them were alone in the great dining room with elaborate hanging tapestries covering the stone walls. He was a large man with a dark and heavy beard, his face with the permanent flush of one who enjoyed too much wine far too often. He sat at a table with a flagon of wine in front of him.

Isabelle sat primly across from her father, her hands folded on her lap in the posture of modesty that she'd been taught since she was a child.

She knew why he was doing this. To make the point that she was wrong to doubt whatever he was going to tell her next. But to mention this would be a sign of insolence. And Lord Mewburn had no patience for insolence in any form. When he reigned over Magnus, he would order a man's tongue to be cut from his mouth with the same lack of hesitation he would display when requesting another flagon of wine.

"The earl's son sent for representatives from the king. Directed by the son, they found letters from the earl, in the earl's handwriting, and sealed in wax with the earl's symbol, in a pouch to be delivered to other earls and lords across the entire kingdom. These letters requested help in overthrowing the king."

Lord Mewburn scratched methodically at his chin through his wiry beard, a habit that Isabelle found irritating. He nodded.

"These letters, of course, and the wax seals were counterfeits, an easy enough task for us," Isabelle continued. "The earl protested his innocence, but based on the testimony of his own son, he was immediately thrown into his own prison."

As she spoke, she wondered if her irritation was rising because of her unhappiness with the situation. Michael, son of the Earl of York, had been placed in a temporary position to oversee the earldom, and soon enough, after the official letter of gratitude from the king, he would be pronounced the new Earl of York. Sacrificing his own ear had indeed been a small price. Betraying one's father—well, that was a higher price, if a man had a conscience, but she doubted Michael did.

Of more concern to Isabelle was that she was expected to wed Michael once he became the new earl, giving her one of the highest places of nobility in all of England. A perfect place for a woman to be able to influence events on behalf of the Druids. Power and wealth would be hers, something she had been bred to desire. But without Thomas at her side...

"Go on," Lord Mewburn said.

"In Magnus," she said, "as we have heard by other messengers, Thomas has gone into hiding from the Priests of the Holy Grail. A bounty has been placed upon his head."

He shall escape, she told herself. She couldn't bear the thought of discovering that Thomas had been captured and tortured, as the earl had been, here in York. This was wrong, she knew, to be hoping that Thomas would escape the power of the Druids.

"And he shall escape," Lord Mewburn said.

For a moment, she wondered if she had spoken her thoughts aloud. She found herself blinking in surprise.

"He shall escape," Lord Mewburn repeated, "because events are unfolding as planned. It will do our battle no good for Thomas to be in a prison in Magnus or hanging from a rope. We want what he has hidden from us. Magnus has only been taken from him to drive him toward us again."

"How can you be so certain he will come here?" Isabelle asked, doing her best to hide her emotions at the thought of seeing Thomas again.

Lord Mewburn steepled his fingers and smiled at her. "Because for centuries we have always been proven correct. But as part of your education, I will explain why in this situation. Thomas will have heard about the earl's imprisonment, and he will be convinced that the earl must be an ally. Thomas will guess that those who have overthrown York are those who have overthrown Magnus. He will want to learn what he can from the earl and, I would also guess, want to try to assist him. It means, of course, that sooner than later, Thomas will arrive here."

"Yes, Father," Isabelle said.

"When he arrives," Lord Mewburn said, "let's make sure you are in a position to offer Thomas what he wants. Are you capable of that?"

Isabelle made sure that she did not show any of the joy that came with the quickening of her heart.

She simply repeated her words. "Yes, Father."

SIXTEEN

SPRING, PARIS, FRANCE—AD 1313

K atherine startled as a shadow crossed the pages of her open book. "I'm sorry, my child," a soft voice reassured her. "The thoughts I interrupted, they must have been enjoyable. Your face showed such pleasure. And I was clumsy to—"

She blushed. "*Frère* Dominic, it is I who should apologize for daydreaming. The progress I have made with my Latin has not been remarkable. With all due respect to the author, it is...it is..."

Katherine fumbled for a tactful way to express how boring she found eleventh-century German philosophy. Her French failed her, however, and all she could do was shrug and look down modestly.

"Katherine," Frère Dominic admonished, "is it not enough you have won an old priest's heart? And now you take advantage of it with beautiful helplessness that is merely acted?"

Katherine laughed. Little escaped the old priest. He moved with the energy of a far younger man. Although he was plump and graying and always wore the smile of a jolly man, his eyes gleamed sharp in unguarded moments—or during the rough-and-tumble arguments in logic he and Katherine enjoyed as a means to pass time throughout the long winter.

"Father?" Katherine asked, searching his eyes. "Is something wrong?"

Frère Dominic nodded. "Only for me," he said. "You see, when I tell you my heart has been stolen, it is not merely the flattery of a man who enjoys too much"—the priest patted his stomach—"your touch with our French recipes. I shall truly miss your presence here."

Katherine stood quickly. She took one of the priest's hands in hers and squeezed it tight. "He has returned?"

Frère Dominic nodded, then shook his head mournfully. "After an absence of six months, he refuses to accept the hospitality of one night's stay here. Even now, that scoundrel is in the stable, preparing a horse for you."

Katherine dropped the priest's warm hand. "Travel? So soon? Did he mention…"

Once again, Katherine blushed.

"England?" Frère Dominic finished for her.

Katherine nodded, watched the priest's face, and waited.

"Yes," he finally said, then smiled at her unconcealed expression. "Your face again carries the look I interrupted moments ago. Who is he that captures your thoughts, Katherine? Were I three decades younger, I would be smitten with jealousy."

SEVENTEEN

Katherine and Hawkwood rode for two days to reach the harbor town of Dieppe on the French side of the English Channel.

She knew Hawkwood was anxious. He did not question the price offered for their horses in Dieppe, although it was scandalously low. And half an hour later, he did not barter with the ship's captain for passage across the Channel.

Three days on the pitched and gray North Sea brought them to Kingston upon Hull. Once again, Hawkwood did not waste time searching for the fairest price of horseflesh and paid double what he should have.

They rode thirty miles, directly to an obscure abbey north and east of the town of York, stopping as they traveled only when the sun went down.

⚜

"Patience," Hawkwood said, "is well known as a virtue."

"Then I shall be nominated for sainthood," Katherine replied. "For nearly a week now, I have waited for you to inform me of the reason for our mad haste."

She waved at the land around them. "And now you ask me to sit here for hours, perhaps days, on the mere chance that Thomas might arrive in this remote valley."

"Keep your hands still," Hawkwood admonished. "He must have no hint of our presence."

"He will not arrive."

Hawkwood chuckled. "Your voice betrays your hope."

To that, Katherine did not reply. For Hawkwood spoke truth.

His earlier promise—and only information—had been that Thomas would arrive. And Hawkwood had never been wrong.

So they had settled into the side of the hill barely a half hour earlier, just as the morning sun rose to show her the valley below. It was narrow and compressed, with more rock and stunted trees on the slopes than sweet grass and sheep.

Although they were near the exposed summit of the valley, Hawkwood had shrewdly chosen a vantage point among the shadows of large rocks.

Lower down, trees guarded the tiny river that wound past the abbey a half mile downstream.

Hawkwood had pointed at a jumble of rocks and boulders on the river, some as large as a peasant's hut.

"There," he had said, "is hidden a dry, cool cave, invisible except to those who have been led to its narrow entrance among the granite and growing bush. It is his destination."

And now, long enough later so that the prickling of the sun's first heat had coaxed out the ants that marched through the dust in front of her, Katherine brought the discussion back to her questions.

"Not only shall I receive sainthood for patience, but if ignorance is bliss, I shall be the happiest saint to have walked this earth."

It drew another chuckle.

"Yes," Hawkwood said. "I tell you little. But for your own protection."

"No," Katherine corrected. "For the protection of Magnus." She then repeated oft-heard words. "After all, I cannot divulge what I do not know."

That drew a sigh.

"Katherine," he said, "not even I know the entire plan. We all have our tasks and must trust to the whole."

Would it be fair, she wondered, to push him now for more?

She hesitated. Was it fair, she countered herself, to know so little?

So she decided to ask, almost with dread at his anticipated anger. "Yes," she said softly. "There is truth in that. You fear that I might be taken by the Druids and be forced to betray us. But if something should happen to you? How could I carry on our battle without more knowledge than I have now?"

Hawkwood dropped his head. Instead of anger, sadness filled his voice. "There is truth in that. And I've wondered how long it would take for you to turn my sword of defense back upon me."

She waited, sensing victory but feeling no enjoyment in it.

He continued. "In the cave below are books. In Latin, French, even Italian. But mostly Latin. Once, as you know, those of us in Magnus had the leisure to translate from all languages into that universal word."

"Books?" Katherine was incredulous. "Here in this valley? But that is treasure beyond value! Why here?"

"Well put," he said. "Treasure beyond value. More than you know. These are not books coveted by the wealthy for beauty and worth. In that cave lies knowledge brought from lands as far away as the eastern edge of the world. All for Thomas to use in his solitary battle."

"That is why you are so certain he will return," Katherine breathed.

"The message told me Magnus has fallen. With no money and no army, he has no choice but to seek power from the knowledge in that cave."

"Much as he did to first conquer Magnus," Katherine said absently.

A sharp intake of breath from Hawkwood. "You know that?"

"His wings. 'The wings of an angel,'" she said simply. "How else could he have had such a secret?"

"Of course," he said. "You would not fail to see the obvious."

Should she feel guilty? Her answer was not a lie, but she had not divulged to Hawkwood that Thomas had once told her of these books. And that he had regretted it later as he banished her from Magnus.

Katherine now realized the immensity of the secret Thomas had held, not knowing she was one of his watchers. But her new information only led to more questions.

"How did the books arrive here? When? Why?"

"The books arrived by horse. Along the path of the Crusades. And that is all I wish to say."

There was a finality to his tone that told her not to pursue those questions further. So Katherine puzzled through more thoughts, then changed the direction of her query. "Why must we continue to watch? Surely he now needs our help."

Hawkwood shook his head. "Not until we are certain to which side he belongs. Our only word was that Magnus has fallen. I had expected a letter from Gervaise to guide us further. Before sending Thomas back here, Gervaise was supposed to test Thomas, to find a way to know, finally, if we can trust him. Yet nothing has arrived from Gervaise. I pray he has only been imprisoned, not killed. For us, in this game of masks behind masks, we can now only wait."

Katherine finished for Hawkwood. It was a familiar argument. "For if Thomas were a Druid, he would act as if he were not. Now, perhaps, it is convenient for them to assume open control of Magnus. And equally convenient for them to send him forth as bait."

He, in turn, finished her oft-used argument. "Yet if he is not one of them, we can do so much good by revealing ourselves. Together, our fight would be stronger. If we could trust him."

"And," she added, "find a way to have him trust us."

They both sighed. It was an argument with no answer. Too much depended on Thomas.

⚜

When he arrived, they almost missed him.

It was obvious he'd spent years avoiding the nearby harsh monks in his boyhood, slipping along every secret deer path in the surrounding hills. At times, Thomas would approach a seemingly solid stand of brush, then twist sideways into an invisible opening among the jagged branches and later reappear quietly farther down the hill.

His familiarity with the terrain, however, did not make him appear less cautious.

It was only the loud caws of a disgruntled crow that warned Katherine and Hawkwood. Even then, it took them twenty minutes to see his slow movement.

From above, they saw Thomas circle the jumbled rocks near the river once. Then he slipped into a nearby crevice and surveyed the area.

"He was taught well," Hawkwood whispered with approval. "He has no reason to be suspicious, yet still he remains disciplined."

Minute after minute passed.

"He counts to one thousand," Hawkwood explained. "He was taught that this cave was the most important secret of all. Taught never to let anyone discover the entrance."

Thomas circled slowly once more, sometimes visible. Sometimes not.

Katherine ached to see his face close, to discover if she still felt as she remembered when she looked into his eyes. But she, too, had been taught discipline and held herself motionless, with nothing of those thoughts crossing her face.

Then she noticed something.

"He walks awkwardly," she whispered. "Not from the bag he carries. But as if hunched."

Then she gasped as that hump on his back moved. And just before Thomas disappeared into the cave, she received a glimpse of his burden as it poked its nose out from the back of his shirt.

"A puppy," she said in amazement. "An entire kingdom rides on his shoulders, and next to it, he carries a puppy?"

Eighteen

T wo days passed.

Yet during the long hours of waiting, Katherine could satisfy little more of her curiosity through discussion. Hawkwood insisted on near-perfect silence. He also insisted on alternating watch duty. One must sleep while the other observed the rocks of the entrance.

The few moments they were both awake were spent sharing the sack of breads and cheeses they had carried with them.

At night they moved closer down to the rocks of the river and settled into a nearby crevice in the hill. They could not trust the light of the moon to remain unclouded, and Thomas might leave at any hour. Twice already he had alarmed them with sudden appearances, only to fill a leather bag with water and return to the cave.

Hawkwood had whispered to Katherine that at night, then, their ears must serve as their eyes, for if they failed to follow Thomas to his next destination, the plan would surely be doomed.

Tell me more of the plan, Katherine had wanted to ask, but did not. She knew her duty, and what Hawkwood knew of the plan would only be revealed when he deemed it proper.

So she sat, shivering in the early hours of the third day. Despite her coldness, the discipline she had been taught since birth did not leave her. She did not let the shivers shake her body. Utterly still, she resembled so closely the rock around her that once a fox almost blundered across her feet. At the last moment, it caught her scent and leaped sideways to disappear into the dark jumbles of trees and rocks.

That was the only break in the monotony. Yet, except for the shivering, Katherine did not mind. In these quiet moments she felt at peace.

Soon, the rhythms of approaching day would begin, telling her that God's order still remained in nature, even amid the confusion of the affairs of men and their struggles that had brought her to this quiet valley. Faint gray would brush the horizon first. Then tentative and sporadic chirps of faraway birds, as if they hardly believed they were to be given the gift of another new day. The rustling of the small night creatures would stop in response.

Each minute of growing light would bring her unexpected pleasures. Yesterday, it had been the careful and delicate stepping of a spider across large beads of dew on its web, across a branch so close to Katherine's face that she could see each drop of water bend, but not quite break, with the weight of the spider. The day before, she'd seen a rabbit, trailed by six tiny bundles of fur, each intent on tumbling exactly into the mother rabbit's footsteps.

Part of Katherine knew that she chose to focus on the hill around her because she wanted relief from the questions she could not yet ask Hawkwood.

She knew his urgency stemmed from those reports that Magnus had once again fallen, and with that, at least, she understood the need for action. Without Magnus... Now that she had been fully taught the history and tradition of the Immortals, she hardly dared contemplate how many centuries of careful guidance were on the brink of destruction.

But why the importance of Thomas? And when could she reveal her role to him?

Deep as her feelings for him might run, warm as the skin on her face might flush as she remembered him, Katherine needed to force herself to remain objective enough to wonder why so much rested upon his shoulders.

Where were the other Immortals of this generation? Must Thomas combat the Druids alone and ignorant of battles that had been fought for centuries?

And why now the extreme urgency? After all, until Thomas had recaptured the kingdom the previous summer, Magnus had been under control of the Druids for twenty years. Surely the passing of a month, two months, could not determine the battle now?

Surely—

"Katherine."

She turned her head slightly to acknowledge she had heard Hawkwood's waking words.

"Day is nearly upon us."

So it was. Despite her determination to contemplate the beauty of creation, those faint licks of gray had been banished by pale blue while her thoughts had wandered to areas that Hawkwood refused to discuss.

Katherine stirred, ready to pick her careful way back to the observation point farther back.

"Wait!" came the soft whisper.

She froze. And immediately understood.

Below her, Thomas had finally moved out of the cave and into sight. Without the sack of food he had carried inside. Without the leather bag for water. Without the puppy.

He wore the plain brown garb of a simple monk.

NINETEEN

They followed him along an isolated path in the forest south of the small Harland Moor Abbey. Katherine and Hawkwood did not follow Thomas together. Rather, Hawkwood remained ahead. It was his duty to melt invisibly into the trees and keep Thomas in sight. Katherine, a hundred yards behind and less adept at stealth, simply kept Hawkwood in her line of vision.

At times, she lost sight of him completely. She marveled again and again at how silently he flitted from tree to tree, bush to bush.

An hour later, Hawkwood held up a hand of warning, then settled into a crouch.

Katherine responded by doing the same.

Five minutes later, Hawkwood was up again and moving ahead. This loose march of three, Thomas unaware and in the lead, continued for another half hour until they reached the road leading into the town of Helmsley.

Hawkwood waited for her at the side of the road.

"He is ahead of us, of course," he told Katherine. "I have no doubt he is going to town, much as we, too, needed to stop there before going to the valley."

Katherine raised an eyebrow in question. "His detour?"

"Gold," Hawkwood replied. "He has retrieved some of the gold he had buried before leaving here with the knight for Magnus last summer. The gold he had earned from the gallows in Helmsley. And gold can only mean he has purchases in mind."

Hawkwood's prediction proved correct.

They next saw Thomas near the Helmsley stables where they had left their own horses a few days earlier. Watching discreetly proved to be no problem, not with the usual crowds around the market stalls.

Thomas engaged himself in conversation with the ruddy-faced fat man who tended the stables.

After five minutes, both nodded. The fat man disappeared inside the stable and returned with a small gray horse.

Thomas shook his head. The fat man shrugged. Another five minutes of conversation, this time with much animated movement of hands by both.

The fat man again entered the stable. This time he returned with a large roan stallion. Even from their vantage point, Katherine could appreciate the power suggested by the muscles that rippled and flinched as the horse occasionally shook itself of flies.

A few more minutes of conversation. A snort of derisive laughter from the fat man reached them. And yet again he entered the stables. He brought out not a horse but shabby blankets and saddlebags customarily placed on donkeys.

Thomas nodded and the fat man departed. Instead of swinging onto the horse, Thomas threw a blanket over it and cinched on the saddlebags. He remained on foot and led the horse away by its halter.

As soon as he was safely out of sight, Katherine and Hawkwood approached the stable man.

Hawkwood flashed a bronze coin.

The stable man grunted recognition. "The two of you." He looked at the coin and sneered. "I thought you'd both died. I've kept both your mounts in oats for three days. You expect that to pay the fare?"

"No," Hawkwood said. He pulled a tiny gold coin from deep within his cloak and handed that to the man.

The fat man bit the coin to test for softness, then said, "It's barely enough, but I'm not one to take advantage of strangers."

"It's a third more than you expected," Hawkwood said quietly. He then showed the bronze coin again. "And this is yours if you tell us what the little sparrow heard."

"Eh?"

Hawkwood fluttered his hand skyward. "The little sparrow flitting around as you spoke to that monk's assistant. What harm could there be in telling us words from a sparrow's mouth?"

The fat man leered comprehension. "Ah, that sparrow. Now I recall." He leaned forward and widened his leer to show dark stumps for teeth. "Unfortunately, that sparrow's a shy one."

A second bronze coin appeared in front of the stable man.

"The monk's assistant told me he wanted a horse that could outrun any in York," the stable man said quickly. "That was all."

"York?" Hawkwood repeated.

"York." The man nodded.

"You spent ten minutes in conversation," Katherine protested. "And that was the entire exchange?"

The stable man looked at her darkly, then back at Hawkwood. "It's a sad day when a woman interrupts the business of men."

Katherine rose on her toes to answer, but caught the slight warning wave of Hawkwood's hand.

"I'll see she learns her lesson," Hawkwood said. He then stroked his chin. "York. Hasn't its earl fallen from power?"

"It's what I said too." The stable man nodded again. "I told him what even the deaf and blind know. The Earl of York now rots in his own dungeon."

The fat man paused.

"Yes?" Hawkwood prompted.

"It's peculiar. When I said that, the assistant told me that's exactly why he needed the horse."

⚜

Katherine knew Hawkwood had no appreciation for foolishness, so she waited an hour to ask her question. By then they had traveled five miles along the road to York. By then she had sifted through enough of her thoughts to know which question to ask. Even if she would not start with it.

"We have not reached nor passed Thomas yet," she began. "This means one of two things."

"Yes?" Hawkwood asked in good humor. Katherine knew it lifted his spirits when she applied her training.

"Either he mounted his horse as soon as he was out of sight of the town and has ridden it fast enough to keep the distance between us as he travels to York. Or—"

"How do you know it will be the second and not the first?" Hawkwood interrupted.

Katherine smiled. "Because he wants to appear as a lowly monk's assistant leading a master's horse from one town to the next. He doesn't dare ride, because too many travel this road, and many would wonder at someone dressed so poorly mounted on such a fine horse. Since we have not yet reached him, he does not first travel to York."

Hawkwood clapped approval. "Instead, he has…"

"Thomas has undoubtedly returned to the abbey to retrieve what he needs from the cave, to fill those saddlebags." Katherine paused at the thought and what it meant. "He is arming himself."

"Yes, my friend." Hawkwood said nothing more, and they passed the next hundred yards with only the *clop-clop* of the horses' hooves to break their companionable silence. A breeze at their backs kept the dust from rising, and Katherine let it lull her thoughts away from her question.

She turned her gaze downward as the minutes passed. Not for the first time did Katherine stare at the road and wonder at the Roman soldiers who had set the stones more than a thousand years earlier, even before the time of Merlin himself. York had been an outpost in the wild interior, Hawkwood had explained five days previous as they had departed Scarborough. Scarborough, forty miles northeast, had been the coastal watch post, and from its high cliffs, the Roman sentries could easily spot enemy ships. The efficient road to the interior made it easy to shuffle legions of soldiers back and forth between Scarborough and York. And now, hundreds of years later, it carried the everyday traffic between the towns along that route.

"Katherine."

She pulled away from her thoughts.

"What question do you have?"

"You can read me that well?" Katherine said.

"You had no need to impress me with your guesses. Except that I am sometimes impatient with meaningless prattle, and it seemed as if you sought to discuss Thomas more."

Katherine felt her face color as she noticed Hawkwood's tiny grin of comprehension and the twinkle in the old man's eyes. He knew too well her thoughts of Thomas.

She also knew Hawkwood did not like false modesty or coy games, so she simply asked her question with no further hesitation.

"Why York?" she blurted. "Thomas knows, as do all, that the Priests of the Holy Grail rule it as surely as they rule Magnus. Why enter the lions' den?"

Hawkwood spoke so softly she could barely hear. "I've wondered that myself. Perhaps he has decided if he frees the Earl of York, they will swear a pact of allegiance and together fight these Holy Grail priests. Perhaps he simply wishes to observe the priests without fear of recognition by the townspeople as would happen to him in Magnus. After all, he knows, as do you, the first maxim of warfare is simple: 'Know thine enemy.'"

Another hundred yards.

The riders swayed to the rhythm of the slow plodding. With less urgency now than during their previous travels, there seemed little purpose in taxing the horses.

The leaves of the oak trees lining the road had already burst from buds. Dappled shade covered them as they moved steady along the road. Soon the leaves would be full and the road would be entirely sheltered from the sun.

Had only four seasons passed since Thomas first entered Magnus? Only four seasons since she had first spoken to him in a candle maker's shop? Only four seasons since his long-predicted arrival had captured her heart?

Another thought haunted her. In another four seasons, would Thomas still be alive and the battle continued?

"Your face is an open book, my friend." The gentle voice once again took her from her thoughts.

"Even if Thomas frees the earl," Katherine blurted, "or if Thomas knows the Priests of the Holy Grail as well as they know themselves, how can he prevail against their miracles? Blood of the martyr. The weeping statue." Katherine resisted the urge to cross herself as peasants did to speak of such sacred things.

"The blood and statue I can explain easily," Hawkwood said shortly after. "How he is to prevail, I cannot."

"Please," Katherine said quietly. "I have great curiosity."

"Simple," Hawkwood said. "The blood that clots and unclots is nothing holier than a mixture of chalk and the water from rusted iron, sprinkled with salt water." He snorted. "Those false priests pray for the congealed blood to turn to liquid, but they help their prayers by gently shaking the vial. That's all it takes. And when it settles, it appears to be thickly clotted blood."

"And the weeping statue?"

Another snort. "Those stone eyes only weep water when brought from the warmth into the coolness of the church. More sham and trickery."

"Thomas could expose those tricks for what they are!" Katherine said. "Surely, if enough see the truth, the priests would be known as frauds and lose their power to rule."

"No, Katherine. There is only one Thomas, and thousands upon thousands to convince, even if he could. People treasure their misconceptions, cling to them, and never look beyond. Besides, how long could Thomas travel as a free man during his demonstrations against the priests?"

Katherine puzzled for several moments. "An army, then. Thomas will observe the Priests of the Holy Grail, discover their weaknesses, and muster an army to strike as he sees best."

The old man shook his head. "With what money might he raise an army? With what allegiances? Moreover, the priests now maintain rule because all believe they are the spokesmen for God. What man, what knight dares raise a sword against the Almighty with false miracles plain to see and so eagerly believed?"

They traveled much farther before Katherine spoke again. "There seems to be little hope for him. For us."

Hawkwood snorted. "Perhaps Thomas is not meant to prevail. I repeat, we still have no certainty to which side he belongs. They must know he is watched by us, even if they do not know the watchers. An apparent defeat of Thomas will lead us to trust him, and with trust, we might impart to him the final secrets they need so badly."

Katherine could only set her chin stubbornly as a means to hold back a sigh of sadness.

The never-ending logic of argument.

She closed her eyes and spoke to the sky. "This waiting is a cruel game."

TWENTY

Their wait at the massive gates to the town wall was rewarded as the bells rang *sext* to mark midday.

Unlike Magnus, the walls around the entire town of York did not have the advantage of a protecting lake. Because of that, they were much thicker to better protect against battering rams. Indeed, so wide were these walls that atop were large chambers built from equally massive stone blocks.

Katherine and Hawkwood were so close to the west gate of York that almost directly above them, and built into the high arch above the entrance to the town, was one of the prisons of York.

An open window had been cut into each of the four walls of the prison, hardly large enough for a small boy to crawl through. Despite that restriction, and despite the sheer thirty-foot drop to the ground, iron bars had been placed into the windows as a final barrier to prisoners with dreams of escape.

When Katherine looked up, she imagined the occasional dark shadow of movement through the window closest to her. She did not look up often, however. Imbedded into the stone walls were iron pikes. Upon three, the heads of three men were impaled, staring their silent horror upon the town as warning to those who might also become rebels.

Mostly, then, Katherine watched a stream of peasants and craftsmen enter the town beneath those gateway prisons. The air was noisy with marketplace shouts and curses.

This steady stream disappeared quickly once inside York as the cobbled road twisted and turned its way inside to dozens of side streets. Those new to the wonders of York stopped almost immediately at one of the shops on the side of the road. The more experienced and unwilling to be fleeced continued toward the markets.

They stood among the jostling people bartering for the wares in the cook shop, positioned to sell to the impatiently hungry. The aromas of the food did not make their waiting easy. Katherine could smell roasted joints and meat pasties—all at a price double what one could expect to pay closer to the town center.

They had taken their spot the previous afternoon, abandoned it with reluctance at sunset when the gate closed, and resumed it at dawn. To amuse herself as she waited, Katherine tested her powers of observation by scanning the crowd for pickpockets.

She saw two. One particularly clever thief played the role of a drunk. He staggered and bounced into people, enduring their abuse and leaving with the coins he had filched during the confusion created by his falling against them.

Yesterday, juggling men tossed whirling swords and flames so adeptly a half hour passed seemingly in the space of a drawn breath. Katherine hoped they would return. Even Hawkwood beside her had coughed admiration and thrown small coins in their direction.

Or perhaps the man with the wrestling bear would entertain again. What a treat that had been. Of course, she told herself, sights such as these were to be expected in York. After all, with its ten thousand inhabitants, only London exceeded it in size.

Katherine lapsed into her favorite daydream, the one where she was able to explain as much as she knew to Thomas. She formed an image of his face and tried not to hear his last words to her as he banished her from Magnus. She tried to picture his smile as he finally understood why she had withheld the truth...

Hawkwood nudged her just as the last of the sext bells rang. "He approaches," came his whisper. "Hide your face well."

⚜

Thomas went no farther than the town gates.

They were close enough to see the expression of surprise on his face as the guard shrugged and pointed upward. They were close enough to see the discreet transfer of a gold coin from Thomas's hand to the guard's. They were close enough to hear Thomas's instructions to a boy standing just inside the town walls.

He left the boy holding the horse's reins and guarding it just inside the town gate. Thomas then spun on his heels and half-sprinted back to the guard beneath the arch of the town wall.

The guard nodded upon his approach, brought Thomas to the side of the arch, and led him through a door.

"Can it be?" Hawkwood said in hushed tones from their viewpoint in the shadows at the side of the cook shop. Then conviction entered his voice. "It must. Why did I not realize it before?"

"Yes?"

He pointed upward. "The Earl of York is held there." He pointed upward. "Not in the sheriff's prison. I, too, should have asked the same question he did upon entering York."

Katherine caught the trace of self-doubt. "No," she said as she patted his arm, "you should not have asked. We did not want to draw attention to ourselves."

Hawkwood sighed. "Of course."

His sadness disturbs me, Katherine thought as they resumed their watch in silence. *He has never allowed me to see it before.*

Following that sigh, none of her former distractions seemed enjoyable, and the waiting and watching passed very slowly.

Three-quarters of an hour later, Thomas stepped outside again, nodded at the guard, and returned to his horse. He took the reins from the boy, and without looking back, led the horse into the center of York.

Even before Thomas was lost to sight in the swirling crowds, Hawkwood pressed two coins into Katherine's hand.

"One to bribe the same guard he did," he explained. "The other to bribe the guard above."

He spoke with renewed vigor. Was it an effort to restore her confidence? She, of course, did not comment. Merely waited for more instructions.

"Reach the earl," he said next. "We must hear what Thomas plans."

"If the earl does not speak?" Katherine asked.

"Tell him it is the only way for him to remove the curse from his family."

Katherine paused. "I do not understand."

"He will," came the reply. "All too well."

TWENTY-ONE

D amp stone steps led upward in a dim, tight spiral. The guard's leering cackle still echoed in Katherine's mind as she began to climb.

"'Tis money poorly spent for an audience, my sweet duckling," he had said. *"The earl's as powerless as a newborn babe."*

Knowledge is power, Katherine told herself firmly, *and if the earl shares his, it will be worth every farthing.*

She reached the open chamber at the top of the stairs. The ceiling was low, and the only furniture was a crude wooden chair for the upper guard as he watched the doors of the four cells that opened into the chamber.

As she arrived, the guard was unlocking one of the doors.

It startled Katherine. *How does he know I wish to visit the earl? I have not yet placed a bribe in his hand nor stated my request.*

Her silent question was answered within moments as she saw a prisoner step through the low opened doorway. That prisoner was not the Earl of York.

"You've done well," the prisoner said to the guard. "It is no surprise that Thomas—"

He stopped suddenly as he noticed Katherine. The guard turned too, and they both stared at their quiet visitor.

The black eyes of the prisoner studied her sharply. His cheeks were rounded like those of a well-stuffed chipmunk. Ears thick and almost flappy. Half-balding forehead, and shaggy hair that fell from the back of his head to well below his shoulders. A thoroughly ugly man.

And she recognized him.

His name was Waleran. He had once shared a dungeon cell in Magnus with Thomas, placed there as a spy to hear every word he spoke. Katherine had been there too, but as a visitor, disguised beneath a covering wrap of bandages around her face.

Katherine bit her tongue to keep from blurting out her surprise at his presence.

Waleran being here meant Thomas had already been discovered, within the hour of arriving in York!

If she, too, were now discovered…

Katherine reminded herself that with her face exposed, she had nothing to fear. This man had seen her only when she was bound in the filthy bandages across her face.

Still, Katherine fumbled for words. "I've brought this for the…the former earl," she said, extending the wrapped food as proof that Hawkwood had insisted she carry. "To repay a kindness he once did my father."

Would Waleran believe her? Katherine bowed her head in a humbleness she hoped hid her flush of fear. In the brief pause as she waited, her heart pounded a dozen times.

How can I warn Thomas? If I leave now, they will suspect me!

The prisoner finally spoke to the guard. "Help this pretty creature. I need no escort. And time presses me."

It is Waleran who orders the guard!

The guard grunted agreement and began to unlock the adjacent door.

Katherine let her pent breath escape slowly as Waleran brushed past her and began to descend the stairs, without a doubt on his way to inform Michael, the new Earl of York, that Thomas was near. She willed herself to move forward slowly, despite the sudden extreme urgency.

The guard blocked her movement. Her heart leaped into her throat. But then the guard held out a grimy hand, and she understood. She had forgotten the bribe. With concealed relief, she placed a coin into his palm. He bowed mockingly and made room for her to enter the prison cell.

Before the door had latched firmly behind her, she started in a rushed whisper.

"My good lord," she began, "there is—"

The former Earl of York no doubt understood why she halted her words.

He touched his face lightly with exploring fingertips of his left hand. "The penalty of losing an earldom. It appears much more terrible than it is," he told her. "There are days I do not feel any pain, and without a reflection…" The earl shrugged.

This was not the proud warrior who had stood beside Thomas in battle against the Scots. This was not the confident man of royalty who had later decreed that Thomas surrender himself and Magnus. Gone was the trimmed red-blond hair that spoke of Vikings among his ancestors. His face was still broad but no longer remarkably smooth. The blue eyes that matched the sky just before dusk were now dimmed. And gone was the posture of a man at ease with himself and the world he commanded.

Instead, his face was crisscrossed with half-healed razor cuts, so that it appeared a giant eagle had raked him repeatedly with merciless talons. His right shoulder hung limp at an awkward angle, popped loose from its socket. And his feet were still in splints, wrapped with bandages mottled gray and red from filth and long-dried blood.

"Please, my dear, smile," he encouraged her. "It would be a small gift well received."

Katherine did so, hesitantly.

He waved her to speak. "You had something to impart, and it seemed with great speed."

Katherine nodded. She did not yet know if she could trust her voice.

She swallowed a few times, then spoke, softly, afraid that her voice would carry to perhaps another prisoner spy.

"Your visitor, Thomas," she said.

The earl leaned forward with a suddenness that made him wince in pain. "You knew the monk's assistant was Thomas of Magnus?"

"Yes, m'lord. Do you see him as an ally still?"

"Yes, of course. I am in this prison because my son betrayed me. And it was my son who fooled me into trying to take Magnus from Thomas. It is a truth that has no comfort in its coldness."

"Then help me," Katherine said, "for I fear those who now hold York will soon learn that Thomas visited you here."

"Impossible," the earl said. "I would not betray Thomas."

Katherine pointed to a vent in the wall. "Impossible that your voices might carry to the prisoner beside you?"

"Hardly," the earl snorted. "My conversations with him have kept me from losing all sanity here. Yet, even if he eavesdropped, there is nothing he can do."

"Unless he were a spy named Waleran." Katherine explained those days with Thomas in the dungeon beneath Magnus.

The earl clenched his fists. "The prisoner across the wall was one of them? A Druid?"

Katherine replied softly. "Then I need not explain the Druid circle of conspiracy?"

The earl shook his head. "No. Nor the darkness they have placed upon my family for generations. You know of the Druids too? What madness is this?"

Katherine nodded at his first question and shrugged at his second. She wanted to ask the questions, instead, to learn what Thomas intended, but she dared not press the earl too quickly.

He shuddered. "Druids. We have always been at their mercy."

He touched a bare finger. "As I told Thomas, I shall tell you. Almost word for word. There was a ring in our family, passed from father to eldest son, the future Earl of York. With it were these instructions: acknowledge the power of those behind the symbol or suffer horrible death. Five generations ago, the Earl of York refused to listen to a messenger—one whose own ring fit into the symbol engraved upon the family ring. Within weeks, worms began to consume his still-living body. No doctor could cure him. Even a witch was summoned. To no avail. They say his deathbed screams echoed throughout the castle for a week. His son—my great-great-grandfather—then became the new Earl of York. When he outgrew his advisors, he took great care in acknowledging the ring that had been passed to him."

This was the family curse Hawkwood meant!

The earl focused his eyes on the floor. "It only meant responding to a favor asked. A command given. Rarely more than one in an earl's lifetime. Sometimes none. My great-grandfather did not receive a single request. Twenty years ago my father...my father stood aside while Magnus fell, despite allegiance and protection promised. He let the new conquerors reign."

He stopped suddenly and darted a sharp look at Katherine. "This is strange, your sudden appearance. You are not one of them?"

She shook her head. "The Druids have already imprisoned you. Why would I be here if I were one of them?"

The earl gaped in sudden comprehension. "These Priests of the Holy Grail are...are...Druids...?"

"And Thomas, I pray, is not," Katherine replied.

The earl shook his head weakly. "First, Thomas with his rash promises. And now you. I feel so old."

"Rash promises?"

"He offered my kingdom back," the earl said.

"What did Thomas ask of you in return?" Katherine asked quickly. "How will he attempt this? Where goes he next?"

The earl stared strangely at Katherine. "It dawns upon me that you are privy to much, yet are a stranger. Why should you have more of my trust? Why should I believe the story of a spy in the cell next door? Perhaps you are here to prevent Thomas from succeeding. After all, only a Druid could know what you do."

The earl gained more strength as his thoughts became more certain. "Only a Druid watcher placed at the gates would have known of Thomas's arrival so soon."

Time—too little time remained. Yet could Katherine betray a secret that had been kept from outsiders for centuries?

She thought of Thomas, of the heads spiked outside this very prison. Even now as she spoke in this dank cell, did Thomas walk unknowingly to his doom? Katherine made her decision.

"Few know of the Druids and the evil they pursue," she whispered. "None know there are those who seek to counter them."

The earl's eyes widened. "Another circle?"

Anguish ripped through Katherine for even hinting at that. Since birth, she had been trained to keep what secrets she knew and had only been permitted to grasp the edges of the truth. It was a secret so precious that not even she knew of much more than the existence of the Immortals, only that she was one of them and had been given much of their teachings.

The earl repeated himself, almost impatiently. "Another circle?"

How could she bring herself to go beyond that hint and betray even more? But there was Thomas. If he were not a Druid but, as she hoped, one like her, mere observation was no longer enough. Thomas now needed help.

Finally, Katherine forced herself to nod. "Yes. Another circle."

Those words hung while she waited until she could remain silent no longer. "Please, Thomas is in danger."

The earl seemed to read the pain in her eyes and spoke. "I gave Thomas my ring," he said, unconsciously twisting his now-bare finger. "He was to offer it at the castle keep as a method to gain an immediate audience with the man who now holds York for the Priests of the Holy Grail. The new Earl of York. My son, Michael."

"That is insane!" Katherine blurted. "For what reason would he seek audience with the enemy?"

The earl's reply stunned her.

"Thomas intends to escape York with a hostage to ransom."

TWENTY-TWO

The sunlight blinded Katherine after the dimness of the prison, and she almost stumbled in her rush to rejoin Hawkwood.

For a moment, she felt panic. Her eyes had adjusted, yet she could not see him in the crowd. Then the familiar black cape appeared as he stepped from a nearby doorway.

His face, always difficult to read, was no different as he approached. Yet Katherine knew he was troubled. Instead of waiting for her information with calmly folded arms, he was reaching out to grasp her shoulders and search her face.

"It is not good," Katherine answered his questioning eyes. "Thomas, it seems, seeks his own death."

She explained quickly.

Later, she would tell Hawkwood what she had had to reveal to the Earl of York to get her news.

"We have little choice but to follow, watch, and pray," Hawkwood said. "Too much happens too soon."

He did not elaborate but turned to march down the street that led to the castle of York.

Katherine remained close behind. Although she did not cast a final look backward, she could not escape the feeling that her every step was watched by the sightless eyes of the heads of the men who had dared rebel against the Priests of the Holy Grail.

❦

They reached the outer courtyard of the castle burdened with a sack of flour that Hawkwood had hurriedly purchased as they had passed by market stalls.

Wolfhounds lazed in the dirt. Servants scurried determined paths through the steady flow of noblemen and ladies who paraded in and out of the entrance with the assured arrogance that money and title provide. Squires stood in conversation with knights casually alert and leaning against stone benches. Other, more humbly dressed squires held the reins of the horses of their masters.

Of Thomas or of Waleran, there was no sign. Within seconds, however, Katherine noticed Thomas's now-familiar stallion tethered to the trunk of a sapling growing in the shadows of the far corner of the court. Tending the horse was the same boy Thomas had hired near the town gate.

She tugged on Hawkwood's arm and whispered, "Thomas is already inside. Do we follow?"

He shook his head no and kept his voice low. "If he succeeds, he must come this way. If not, we will bribe servants to tell us the story of his failure and make our plans in accordance."

"How can he hope to succeed?" Katherine asked.

"That is my question also," Hawkwood said softly. He motioned with his head for Katherine to stay at his side and then walked to the boy who tended Thomas's horse.

"The monk's assistant," Hawkwood said to the boy. "Has he promised to return soon?"

"'E made a jest," the boy replied. "'E said soon, or not a' all."

Katherine shivered. It seemed so futile, this direct attack of a single person. What could Thomas accomplish without an army?

"We have business to complete," Hawkwood continued as he pointed at the sack of flour that Katherine held. "Yet if he trusted you with his horse, he most surely will trust you with his purchase that we now deliver."

The boy shrugged.

"Find an empty saddlebag," Hawkwood instructed Katherine. "We shall leave it there as he requested."

Katherine complied, as puzzled now as when Hawkwood had bought the flour. When she finished, Hawkwood moved beside her to inspect.

"Keep the boy's attention," he said quietly into her ear.

Before Katherine could think of anything to say or do, Hawkwood rejoined her and they strolled to another portion of the court. Little attention fell upon them. The noblemen and ladies, Katherine noted, were much too full of themselves and their gossip to look beyond at mere townspeople.

"All that remains is the wait," Hawkwood said. "And the longer it takes, the less his chances."

Katherine closed her eyes and summoned the vision of her last meeting with Thomas. *"I am sorry, m'lady,"* Thomas had said before banishing her. He had lifted her hand from his arm, then took some of her hair and wiped her face of tears. *"I cannot trust you. This battle—whatever it might be—I fight alone. Please depart Magnus."*

Those were the words that echoed now: *"I fight alone."*

TWENTY-THREE

I t was at least five minutes before Hawkwood spoke again. "He leaves the entrance now."

Katherine opened her eyes wide. And drew her breath in sharply.

For at Thomas's side was another, a person she recognized instantly.

Slim body, long dark hair, haunting half smile of arrogance, now touched with fear. Isabelle Mewburn. The daughter of the former lord of Magnus. Isabelle Mewburn. Who had once proclaimed love for Thomas as a means to assassinate him.

Katherine could not help but feel a stab of jealousy. She knew that Thomas had once been captivated by that royal grace and the stunning features of a fine, pale face. And now, clothed in a dress that made the ladies around her look like shabby peasants, Isabelle seemed more heart winning than ever.

To a casual observer, it might appear that Isabelle merely accompanied the lowly monk's assistant. Yet as Thomas descended the steps at Isabelle's side, Katherine could see strain etched across her face and the falseness of the smiles she offered passersby. For Thomas discreetly had hold of her elbow with his left hand. His right hand was hidden beneath his cape.

Katherine guessed he held a dagger and that he had threatened her life at the slightest attempt of escape, the slightest attempt of obstruction by any of the castle guards. Yet with her dead, Thomas would surely be killed as well.

He was that desperate—that ready to gamble his life.

They reached the courtyard ground.

At the top of the stairs appeared two guards, watching closely every move that Thomas made. They followed from ten yards behind.

Thomas guided Isabelle to his horse. The boy removed the reins from the tree and placed them across the horse's neck.

Isabelle balked as Thomas gestured upward, then slumped as he said something Katherine was unable to hear. A renewed threat to plunge the dagger deep?

She swung up onto the horse.

At that, the idle chatter in the courtyard stopped as if cut by the knife Thomas most certainly held.

"How strange, how crude," the whispers began, "a royal lady mounting a horse in full dress."

Some pointed, and all continued to stare.

Isabelle remained slumped in defeat. Until Thomas moved to climb up behind her. At the moment his grip shifted on the unseen dagger, she kicked the horse into sudden motion.

Thomas slipped, then clutched at the saddle.

His dagger fell earthward.

The next moments became a jumble. Thomas strained to pull himself onto the now galloping horse. Isabelle kicked at his face, and both nearly toppled from the horse. People threw themselves in all directions to avoid the thundering hooves.

And the following guards noticed the dagger lying in the dust.

Free now to act, the first one shouted. "Stop him! He kidnaps the lord's daughter!"

Knights scrambled to their horses. Screams and shouts added to the general panic.

Thomas now had his arms around Isabelle's waist. The horse was galloping in frenzied circles, once passing so close to Katherine that a kicked pebble struck her cheek.

It was his only saving grace, the speed of the horse. Had its panic not been so murderous, Isabelle could have thrown herself free. Instead, she could now only cling to the horse's neck.

Thomas finally reached a sitting position in the saddle and roared rage as he reached for the flapping reins. His hands found one, then the other.

"Raise the drawbridge!" the other guard shouted. "Call ahead and tell them to raise the drawbridge!"

Thomas pulled the reins. The horse responded instantly to the bit. Thomas spun the horse in the direction of the courtyard entrance, then spurred it forward amid the shouting and confusion.

People once again scattered, except for a solitary knight with a two-handed grip on a long broadsword. The knight braced to swing as the horse approached him.

That iron will cleave a leg! Katherine wanted to scream.

As the horse reached, then began to pass the knight, arrows flew. Three whizzed above Thomas and stuck into the stone wall of the courtyard. The last struck the knight's right shoulder, and he dropped in agony. The sword clattered to the ground, useless.

Thomas swept through the gateway and thundered toward the drawbridge.

Katherine scrambled with all the other people in the courtyard to catch a glimpse of what might happen next.

Thomas and the horse passed into the shadows of the gateway.

Already, the bridge was a third of the way raised!

Yet Thomas did not slow the horse. A clatter of hooves on stone, then on wood. Then silence as the horse leaped skyward from the rising bridge and landed safely on the other side of the moat. In the hush of disbelief that followed, that sudden silence became a sigh.

Almost immediately, the thundering of more hooves broke the sigh of silence.

Four knights had finally readied their horses, and the first charged through the courtyard gate toward the drawbridge.

After seeing Thomas escape, Katherine had relaxed. Now, with a deadly group of four in pursuit, Katherine clenched her fists again and for the first time felt the pain. In her fear, she had driven two fingernails through the skin of her palm, and in the heat of action, she had not noticed.

Katherine forced her hands to open again and ignored the tiny rivulets of blood. She could not stop the urge to draw huge lungs full of air, as if she, not Thomas, were in full flight.

Thomas must escape. Yet we are so helpless.

She spun sideways in shock to hear Hawkwood softly laughing.

"Look!" He pointed from their vantage point at the front of the gathered crowd. "The drawbridge."

All four horses skidded and skittered to a complete stop in the archway at the drawbridge. One bucked and pawed the air in fear.

For the huge wooden structure was still rising!

Loud bellows of enraged knights broke the air.

"Fools! Winch it down!"

Hawkwood's delighted chuckle deepened. "Such a bridge weighs far too much to be dropped. They'll have to lower it as slowly as it was raised. With three roads to choose on the other side and open fields in all directions, Thomas will have made good his escape!"

Five minutes later, when the drawbridge was finally in place again, they saw the obvious confusion of the knights as they pranced in hesitant circles at the crossroad beyond the moat.

Hawkwood touched her arm.

"Much has yet to be done," he said. "But if he truly is one of us, we could not ask for more."

Katherine tried to smile.

Yes, she could exult that Thomas still lived. And still lived in freedom.

But he was not alone. And it was not she but another at his side.

TWENTY-FOUR

O ur friend Thomas is free," Hawkwood said. "Yet there is much that troubles me."

Katherine watched his features closely. *There is much that troubles me too. I cannot shake my last vision of him. The reins in his hands. The stallion in full flight. And her...far too beautiful, and Thomas behind her on that horse, holding her far too tight.*

Katherine did not voice those thoughts. Instead, she said simply, "I am sorry you are troubled."

They stood at the crossroads outside the town walls of York. Behind them lay the confusion and chaos of an entire population buzzing with the incredible news. The lord's daughter has been taken hostage! Kidnapped in daylight beneath the very noses of the courtyard knights!

Those same knights had already scattered in all directions from the crossroads where Hawkwood and Katherine and a handful of travelers now stood, each knight engaged in useless pursuit of a powerful horse long since gone on roads that would carry no tracks.

Hawkwood, however, had his head bent even lower now as he searched the hard ground of the well-traveled roads.

"Stay with me," he said softly, leading the horses. "We shall talk as we follow Thomas."

"Follow Thomas?" Katherine echoed with equal softness. "Half an army runs in circles of useless pursuit. If he has escaped them, most surely he has also escaped us."

Hawkwood laughed quietly. "Hardly, my child. Do you not remember the puppy he left behind with his secret treasure of books?"

Of course. In the excitement of his escape, Katherine had allowed herself to forget that Thomas must soon return to the cave that held those books.

"Yes," she said quickly. "We shall find him there. We know he'll have to get back to his books within several days. After all, regardless of his plans, he will not let the puppy die of starvation."

Hawkwood continued his low chuckle. "That only demonstrates that once again when you think of Thomas, you think with your heart. You wish him to have the nobleness of mind that would not let an innocent animal die a horrible death."

"It is otherwise?" Katherine challenged, even though her face flushed at Hawkwood's remark.

"Perhaps not. But others might believe Thomas will return to his puppy merely because of the more valuable books nearby."

Katherine ignored that. "So we proceed back to the valley of the cave and wait."

"Not so," Hawkwood replied. "That is far too long, and time is now too precious."

"Until then?" Katherine asked. She did not want to think about the days Thomas would pass in the company of such an attractive hostage, one who had once claimed a true love for Thomas.

"We will find Thomas by nightfall," Hawkwood promised. His head was still down, and he still examined the ground carefully.

"That shows much confidence."

"No," Hawkwood said, smiling. "Foresight."

Hawkwood grinned triumph and then hurried ahead on the road that led northeast to Scarborough on the North Sea.

Several minutes later, Hawkwood stopped and dropped his voice to a whisper.

"Speak truth now," he warned. "An hour back, in York, you were convinced I had lost my mind to purchase that sack of flour in the midst of our hurry to reach Thomas in the lord's courtyard before he could attempt to take his hostage."

"I-I…," Katherine stammered.

"Answer enough."

Hawkwood tapped the ground at his feet with the end of his cane.

"There," he said. "Our trail to Thomas."

He rubbed the tip of his cane through a slight dusting of coarse unmilled flour.

Katherine nodded, unable to hide her own sudden smile at Hawkwood's obvious delight in himself and at the implications of that flour. After all, in the courtyard had she not distracted the keeper of Thomas's horse while Hawkwood loaded that flour into a saddlebag?

"Yes," Hawkwood said as if reading her mind, "I cut a small hole in his saddlebag, and of course, in the sack of flour. Unmilled and still coarse, the flour that falls through is heavy enough to leave a trail wherever he goes."

A mile farther, Katherine remembered Hawkwood's words at the crossroads.

"What troubles you about the freedom Thomas so dangerously earned?" she asked.

Hawkwood's eyes searched ahead for the next traces of flour as he walked. He answered without pausing in his search.

"Thomas should never have escaped York."

"God was with him, to be sure," Katherine agreed.

"Perhaps," Hawkwood said a step later, "but I suspect instead the Druids in York provided earthly help."

"He nearly lost his life," Katherine protested.

"Are you certain? Describe the events you recall."

Were not the subject matter so serious, Katherine might have enjoyed this test of logic. Somewhere in those events were clues Hawkwood had noticed and now wanted her to find. She summoned vivid memories.

"He left the castle with Isabelle, a dagger hidden beneath his cloak and pressed against her ribs."

"Before that," Hawkwood said with a trace of impatience.

"A boy watched his horse at the side of the courtyard."

"Katherine..." Now his voice held ominous warning.

Suddenly she understood. And understanding brought a pain, as if her heart had twisted in her chest.

"On his arrival," Katherine said slowly, "he met with the Earl of York. A spy in the neighboring cell overheard their entire conversation. That spy then hurried away as I entered the prison."

"Continue," Hawkwood said. Satisfaction in her perception had replaced his rumblings of vexation.

"Much time passed as the Earl of York told me what Thomas intended," Katherine said. "Enough time for the spy Waleran to reach the castle and provide warning."

Katherine's heart twisted more at the implication.

With that much warning, how had Thomas succeeded? Unless those at the castle had not feared his actions. Unless he were one of them.

Another memory flashed. Of a knight blocking escape, with his huge broadsword raised high to cleave Thomas dead as the horse and its two riders galloped toward him. Until a stray arrow slammed through the knight's shoulder.

"It was no accident, then," she said slowly, "that those arrows missed Thomas and instead struck the one knight able to stop him."

"Or," Hawkwood added, "that the drawbridge was not raised enough to hold him inside the town. Then raised high enough to keep the knights from immediate pursuit."

"Yet why?" Katherine moaned. Her words, however, were only meant as release for the sorrow that gripped her. She already knew the answer.

"Our much-used argument," Hawkwood said. "The unseen Druid masters play a terrible and mysterious game of chess. Would they not prepare for any of us who had followed Thomas? The only thing they could not know is that you would recognize Waleran. And neither, of course, could he know you, for bandages no longer cover your face. And had you not seen Waleran and known they had been warned, this escape would not have been suspicious."

"I've always said it could not be," Katherine murmured. "I could not argue with my heart. But a contrived escape can only prove he is one of them..."

Hawkwood stopped and touched her arm in sympathy. It was a touch as light as the breeze that followed them down the road.

"Against the Druids, nothing is what it appears to be," Hawkwood said. "They know we watch, even if they know not who we are. The more it would seem Thomas is not one of them, the more likely we might finally tell him the truth."

They walked farther in silence.

"What shall we do?" Katherine despaired.

"We shall play this mysterious chess game to the end," Hawkwood said grimly. "We shall tell Thomas enough for him to believe we have been deceived. And arrange a surprise of our own. He shall soon be a pawn that belongs to us."

TWENTY-FIVE

That night, Katherine paused in the edge of darkness just outside the glow of light given by the flickers of a small fire in front of Thomas and his captive.

Thomas had chosen his camp wisely. He was flanked on two sides by walls of jagged rock that afforded protection yet did not trap him. The light of his fire was low enough that intruders passing even within twenty yards would not notice, and his horse, tethered to a nearby tree, had been muzzled so it could not betray them with noise.

Katherine had prepared herself to remain cold of heart for this moment. She had told herself again and again since leaving York that she would not care how Thomas had chosen to react to his hostage. What would it matter if she would step into the firelight and find the two gathered together side by side to seek warmth against the night chill, Isabelle's long hair soft against Thomas's face as she leaned on his shoulder?

It would matter, Katherine discovered as her heart seemed to soar upward while she surveyed their makeshift camp. For they were not together, and much as she was forced to suspect Thomas was one of the false sorcerer Druids, it filled her with relief to discover them far apart.

Thomas was seated on a log, leaning with two hands on the hilt of a sword propped point-first into the ground, and staring into the flames. He seemed oblivious to Isabelle on her blanket at the side of the fire. Isabelle's hands were tied together and her feet hobbled no differently than it might have been done to a common donkey.

Hardly the signs of romance!

Katherine smiled, then felt immediately guilty for rejoicing in someone else's misfortune. *Besides,* she reminded herself severely, *we are forced to believe Thomas is one of them.* Another thought stabbed her. *Even if he were one of us, is there surety his heart belongs to me as mine already does to him? Did he not once banish me from Magnus?*

So she set her face into expressionless stone and stepped forward. He would not get the satisfaction of seeing any delight in her manner.

At her movement into the light, Isabelle shouted at Katherine. "Flee! He has set a trap!"

In the same moment, Thomas stood abruptly and slashed sideways with his sword.

Both actions froze Katherine, and a thought flashed through her mind. A warning from Isabelle. They had expected an intruder!

Katherine was given no opportunity to ponder. A slap of sound exploded in her ears, and a giant hand plucked her skirt at her ankles and yanked her upward. Within a heartbeat, Katherine was helpless, upside down and flailing her hands at air, skirt and ankles bound so tightly that she couldn't move her legs.

She bobbed once, then twice, then came to a rest, her head at least five feet from the ground.

She swung upside down gently, and Thomas came forward to examine her.

Wonder and shock crossed his face.

"You!" he said.

"This intruder is an acquaintance?" Isabelle asked, her voice laced with scorn.

Thomas turned and replied patiently, as if instructing a small child. "Your voice is like a screeching of saw blades. Please grace me with silence, unless you choose to answer my questions."

He turned back to Katherine. His face now showed composure.

"Greetings, m'lady." He bowed once, then gestured above her. "As you can plainly see, an arrival was not entirely unexpected. My traitorous captive, however, hoped to give you warning."

Katherine crossed her arms to retain her dignity. It was not a simple task, given the awkwardness of holding a conversation while blood drained to fill her head. "You may release me," she said. "I have no harmful intentions."

"Ho, ho," Thomas said. A smile played at the corners of his mouth. "You just happened by? It was mere coincidence that my saddlebag contains a nearly empty bag of flour?"

Thomas tapped his chin in mock thought. "Of course. You found a trail of flour and hoped to gather enough to bake bread."

"Your jests fall short," Katherine snapped. "Are they instead meant as weapons in your bag of tricks?"

"You approve, then, of the hidden noose attached to a young sapling?" He obviously savored her helplessness. "All one needs do is release the holding rope with a well-placed swing of the sword, and the sapling springs upward."

The expression on his face became less jovial, his voice slightly bitter. "Another weapon from the faraway land of Cathay. Surely you remember our discussion of that matter in better times. Times of friendship."

Katherine regarded Thomas silently and bit her tongue to keep from replying. This oaf knew so little about the risks she had taken and the sacrifices she had made on his behalf. *How could I ever have dreamed of confiding in him! Even if he offered me half a kingdom, I would not tell him the truth.*

"Without speech now?" Thomas suddenly became serious with anger. "Magnus has fallen, and like magic, you appear, dogging my footsteps when I have avoided all the soldiers of York. From you, too, I demand answers."

"Thomas, Thomas," another voice chided from behind him. "Emotion clouds judgment."

He whirled to face a figure in black, head hidden by the hood of the dark gown.

"And you! The old man at the gallows!" Thomas said hoarsely. He raised his sword. "I shall end this madness now."

The figure said nothing.

"Before, I had questions," Thomas continued, the strain of holding back his rage obvious in his voice. "And you spoke only of a destiny. Then disappeared."

Thomas advanced on the figure and threatened with his sword. "Now speak. Give me answers or lose your head."

Still no reply.

Thomas prodded the figure with his sword. It collapsed into a heap of cloth.

"You have much to learn," Hawkwood said from the nearby darkness. "Had I chosen, you could have died a dozen different ways already."

Thomas sagged.

Katherine felt the stirrings of pity for what must be going through him. Anger. Confusion. Desperation. An entire gauntlet of emotions. He must feel intensely weary.

"Accept by the knowledge you are still alive that we come in peace." Hawkwood's voice drifted across the shadows. "Cast your sword aside, and we will discuss matters that concern us both. Or the crossbow I have trained upon your heart will end any hope of conversation."

Thomas straightened and regained his noble bearing. Then he dropped his sword.

Hawkwood stepped into view from the side of the camp. Unarmed.

He shrugged at the expression that crossed Thomas's face. "No crossbow. A bluff, of course. You are free to grasp your sword. But I think your curiosity is my best protection."

Thomas sighed. "Yes." He pointed to the clothes on the ground. "How was it done?"

Katherine coughed for attention. Men! Her eyeballs might pop from her head at any moment and they were more concerned with boasting of techniques of trickery.

"Simple," Hawkwood replied. "It is merely a large puppet, a crude frame of small branches within the clothes, held extended from string at the end of a pole. With the darkness around it to hold the illusion. Easy enough, to throw one's voice."

Katherine coughed louder.

Thomas ignored her and nodded admiration at Hawkwood. "A shrewd distraction."

Hawkwood shrugged modestly. "You are not the only one with access to those books."

Thomas froze at the implications. "Impossible!"

"No?" Hawkwood moved to a log near the fire and sat down. "Please, release poor Katherine. And I shall tell you more. And then, perhaps, you can convince me that kidnapping Isabelle is an action that means we can finally trust you."

Thomas retrieved his sword, stepped out of the low firelight, and approached Katherine where she hung.

He brought his sword back quickly, as if to strike her. A half smile escaped him at her refusal to flinch.

Barbaric scum. To think I once dreamed of holding you. Katherine did not give Thomas the satisfaction of letting him see her thoughts cross her face.

He slashed quickly at the rope holding her feet, and she dropped, headfirst.

It forced from her a yelp of fright.

Yet somehow he managed to drop his sword and catch her in one swift movement that cost him merely a grunt of effort.

For a heartbeat, she was there, in his arms, her face only inches from his. And for that heartbeat, she understood why dreams of him had haunted her since banishment from Magnus.

She could not, of course, see the calm gray of his eyes in the darkness of night, but the depth of those eyes remained clear in her memory. She could feel the warmth of his breath as he strained with the effort of holding her.

The face that looked upon her was, even in the shadows, as she had remembered each morning upon waking. Her right arm had draped around his shoulder as she fell, and the back of her hand brushed his dark hair.

And in the heartbeat of stillness between them, she could sense a strength of quiet confidence, as if he were as muscled as the strongest of knights.

The total impression in that brief moment was much too enjoyable, so the rush of warmth she could not prevent as he held her became an anger. This man had coldly banished her from Magnus. He conspired with the Druids. She should not feel what she did to be in his arms.

Her response at the anger she felt toward herself—almost before she realized her left arm was in motion—was to slap him hard across the face.

He blinked, then set her down gently, but he did not take his eyes from her face.

Katherine glared at him, shook the cut rope loose from her ankles, then strode over to rejoin Hawkwood.

Side by side, they faced Thomas across the tiny fire.

"You promised to tell me more," Thomas said. "And for that, I would be in your debt."

He rubbed his face before continuing. "Although it will take much to convince me of good intentions. And your arrival here was not coincidence. Little encourages me to believe you will speak truth."

How can he pretend so well to be innocent? What monstrous deceit!

Just once, Katherine wished she had not been taught to hold her emotions in control. Just once, she wished she could stamp the ground in frustration and scream between gritted teeth.

Katherine was conscious, however, that Isabelle, still hostage and motionless nearby, was watching her closely. Too closely. So Katherine composed herself to stand in relaxed grace.

Hawkwood answered Thomas.

"We do have much to explain," he said. "There was our first meeting at the gallows—"

Thomas interrupted. "Timed to match the eclipse of the sun. I wish, of course, an explanation for that."

Hawkwood nodded. "Then our midnight encounter as you marched northward to defeat the Scots—"

"With your vague promises of a destiny to fulfill. That, too, you must explain."

"And finally," Hawkwood continued as if Thomas had not spoken, "Katherine's return to Magnus and her instructions from me, which resulted in the trial by ordeal that you survived so admirably."

Thomas shook his head slowly.

"You did not survive?" Hawkwood said in jest. "I see a ghost in front of me?"

"Hardly," Thomas answered with no humor. "You spoke the word 'finally.' There is much more I need to hear. How do you know of my books? What do you know of the Priests of the Holy Grail? Why the secret passages that riddle Magnus? How did you find me in York?"

Thomas paused and delivered his next sentence almost fiercely. "And what is the secret of Magnus?"

Hawkwood shrugged. "I can only tell you what I know."

"Of burning water?" Thomas asked.

Neither Katherine nor Hawkwood was able to hide surprise, even in the low light given by the small flickers of flame.

Thomas pressed. "Of Merlin and his followers?"

Hawkwood sprang forward over the fire and grabbed Thomas by the elbow.

"I advise discretion," he whispered in a hoarse voice. "Your hostage is still a danger to you."

TWENTY-SIX

How many times have I done this? Katherine wondered as she stirred her gruel over the open fire. The small pot before her was dented from dozens of similar mornings over dozens of similar fires during her previous travels with Hawkwood.

Only this morning was different.

Across the fire, instead of Hawkwood resting in thoughtful contemplation of the day, the captured daughter of a powerful lord sat, staring at her with open hostility.

Katherine smiled to herself. At least she was not the only one who received those angry stares. Thomas, too, was marked for hatred by Isabelle's sullen rage.

Not for the first time since rising with the sun's light did Katherine glance at Thomas as he rested against a tree. *Even in the lowly clothes of a monk's assistant, he still appears as noble as the lord of Magnus he once was.*

She quickly turned her head back to the fire. *Stupid child,* she told herself, *appearances are deadly illusions.*

She absently tried to lift the pot away, then sucked in a breath of pain as the hot metal punished her for her lack of concentration.

How much did Thomas now know? If only Hawkwood had not insisted on speaking with Thomas privately last night. If only Isabelle had not been nearby so that they had been forced to walk far from camp and leave her behind as guard over the lord's daughter.

Katherine consoled herself with the thought that it would all be explained later, when Thomas was fully in their control. For as Hawkwood had promised, a surprise for him, that cold-hearted deceiver truly did wait ahead.

⚜

"The girl is expensive baggage," Hawkwood said as Thomas began to roll up the blankets of camp and pack his saddlebags.

"I agree." Thomas snorted. "However, it was your decision to travel with Katherine. And mine to depart from you both."

He looked sideways and grinned to see if his jest had struck the mark. Katherine said nothing but doubted she could hide the tiny flushed circles of anger that she felt burning on her cheeks.

Isabelle laughed, but a dark look from Thomas cut her short.

"Merely as a hostage," Thomas said, answering Hawkwood's original question, "the lord's daughter is worth a fortune. To me, however, she is even more valuable. Small as the chance is, her captivity is my only hope to reclaim Magnus."

"Oh?" Hawkwood queried politely.

It was a deceptive tone, for Katherine had discovered often his mild words were only a prelude to slashing observations that would destroy the most carefully laid argument.

"Soon she will tire of her silence."

"Oh?"

"Her father rules York through Michael, only by permission of the Priests of the Holy Grail, so I am not fool enough to believe that the possibility of her death will frighten the priests into relinquishing power. But she has knowledge of those priests and knowledge of the secret circle of Druids. Not until Isabelle tells me all can I find their weakness or a way to begin to fight."

"Alone?"

"Despite what you said last night, I have been counseled not to place my trust in anyone."

Hawkwood shrugged. "You still need help. Help that we can give."

"I prefer to trust no one. After Isabelle speaks, she will then be ransomed for gold. That, along with what I have now, will fund a small army. And, as you know, I am not without hidden sources of strategy."

"She is still expensive baggage," Hawkwood commented. "Whatever knowledge she gives you is useless. Whatever army you build is useless. And whatever means of fighting you devise is useless."

Thomas tied down the last saddlebag. "For what you told me last night, I am grateful, if indeed it was truth. As for your advice this morning, I thank you too, but, with deference to your age, I must respectfully disagree."

He pulled Isabelle roughly to her feet and tied a rope from her bound wrists to the saddle.

"I am to walk?" she asked in disbelief.

"There are times when chivalry must be overruled by common sense," Thomas said. "You once planned to kill me. I hardly intend to let you control the saddle while I walk."

Thomas swung upward into his saddle. They were ready to depart. Thomas looked at Hawkwood and studiously ignored Katherine.

"Thomas," Hawkwood said, "no amount of force will defeat the Priests of the Holy Grail. Not now. As kings receive their power because all people believe they have a divine right to rule, so now do these priests begin to conquer the land. By the will of the people, they deceive."

Thomas froze, only briefly, but enough to show he had suddenly comprehended.

"Yes," Hawkwood continued. "Is it not obvious? Think of how Magnus fell. By consent of the people inside. None dare argue with signs that seem to come from God, no matter how false you and I know those signs to be. First York, then Magnus. Word has reached me that four other towns have been infiltrated, then conquered by these priests. Soon all this part of England will belong to them. How long before the entire land is in their control?"

Hawkwood paused.

What had they discussed last night? Katherine wondered. This sounded like a plea for Thomas to return to them, to join with them and learn the truth behind Magnus, to help in a final battle against the Druids.

Katherine did not discover the answer.

A loud trumpet shrilled through the forest, and within moments, the trees around them were filled with the movement of dozens of men, on foot and on horseback, crashing toward them with upraised swords.

She relaxed.

The surprise has arrived as arranged, she thought in triumph. *Thomas will now be our pawn, regardless of his answer.*

Then she cried with horror. These were not the expected visitors! The attackers plunging toward camp wore the battle colors of York.

Two lead horses galloped through the camp, scattering the ashes of the fire in all directions. Each rider reined hard and pulled up abruptly beside Thomas and Isabelle.

Within moments, the rest of the camp seemed flooded with men. Some in full armor. Some merely armed with protective vests and swords.

Katherine felt rough hands yank her shoulders. She knew there was little use in struggle and quietly accepted defeat. A man on each side held her arms.

Her attention had been on Thomas.

Now she squirmed slightly to look around her for Hawkwood.

The slight movement earned her an immediate prod in the ribs.

"Pretty or not, m'lady, you'll get no mercy from this sword," came the warning voice in her ear.

Katherine stared straight ahead and endured the arrogant smile that curved across Isabelle's face. Isabelle opened her mouth to speak, but the knight interrupted.

"Greetings from your father," the first knight said to Isabelle. "He will delight to see you safe."

"And you, I am sure, will delight in the reward," she said scornfully as her attention turned to the warrior on his horse.

The knight shrugged.

"Shall my hands remain tied forever?" Isabelle asked.

The knight nodded to one of the men on foot, who stepped forward and carefully cut through her bonds.

Thomas, still in his saddle, had not yet spoken nor moved. His eyes remained focused on Katherine.

Rage and venom. She could feel both from Thomas as surely as if he had spoken those two words.

Yet it was she who should be filled with venom and rage. He had lured them here and sprung this trap to capture them. But the shock of the sudden action had numbed her, and she was still far from the first anger of betrayal. A part of her mind wondered about Hawkwood somewhere behind her, surely just as pinned and helpless as she.

Their capture might end what hopes there had been to defeat the Druids. Would Hawkwood see this as a total defeat? Was he, like her, just beginning to realize the horror that waited ahead? For neither would reveal their secrets willingly. And both knew well the cruelty of torture that delighted the Druids. Katherine prayed she would die quickly and without showing fear.

"We have them all," the second knight grunted to the first knight beside him. "The girl and her old companion."

He then spoke past Katherine's shoulder. "Someone see that the old man reaches his feet. We have no time to waste."

Reaches his feet?

This time Katherine ignored the point of the sword in her ribs and turned enough to see a heap of black clothing where Hawkwood lay crumpled and motionless.

"Sire, he does not breathe!" protested a nearby foot soldier.

"Who struck him down?" the second knight roared. "Our instructions were—"

The first knight held up a hand to silence him.

"It was I," the first knight said quietly. "He leaped in my path, and my horse had no time to avoid him. I believe a hoof struck his head."

No! Katherine wanted to scream. *Impossible!*

For until that moment, she still had held no fear. Hawkwood had been her hope. He would devise a means of escape, even from the most secure dungeon. *He cannot be dead. For if he is, so am I.*

The second knight dismounted, walked past Katherine, and knelt beside Hawkwood. He leaned over and checked closely for signs of life.

"Nothing," the knight said in disgust. "We shall be fortunate if our own heads do not roll for this."

He straightened, then glared at the men holding Katherine. "Bind her securely," he said. "But harm not a single hair. Her life is worth not only yours, but that of every member of your family."

Katherine could not see beyond the blur of her sudden tears. Rough rope bit the skin of her wrists, but she did not feel the pain. Within moments, she had been thrown across the back of a horse, but she was not conscious of inflicted bruises.

Hawkwood was dead. And Thomas and Isabelle were to blame.

TWENTY-SEVEN

"Sit her up properly," barked a voice that barely penetrated Katherine's haze of anguish. "She'll only slow our horses if you leave her across the saddle like a sack of potatoes."

Fumbling hands lifted and propped her in a sitting position and guided Katherine's hands to the edge of the saddle. She was too far in her grief to care, too far to fight.

Her mind and heart were so heavy with sorrow that when her tear-blinded eyes suddenly lost all vision, it took her a moment to realize that someone had thrown a hood over her eyes.

Totally blind, she now had no chance to attempt escape on the horse they had provided her.

Then came a sharp whistle, and her horse moved forward slowly. Each step took her farther away from the final sight she would carry always in her mind, that of Hawkwood silent and unmoving among the ruins of camp.

Eventually, the tempo quickened and the steady plodding of her horse became a canter. Katherine had to hold the front edge of the saddle tight with her bound hands and sway in rhythm to keep her balance.

She could hear her own breathing rasp inside the hood as she struggled to keep her balance in the total darkness that blinded her.

By the slow drumming of hooves, she knew other horses were now beside her, instead of front and back, and from that she knew the trail had widened. Soon, they would be at the main road that led into York.

How far, then?

She and Hawkwood—she felt sharp pain twist her stomach to think of him—had walked several hours along the main road yesterday. That meant less than an hour on horseback to York. There… She shut her mind. To think of what lay ahead was to be tortured twice—now and when it actually occurred. And once would be too much.

Would she have a chance to make Thomas pay for his treachery? Even if it was only an unguarded second to lunge at him and rake her nails down his face? Or a chance to claw his eyes?

The cantering of the horses picked up pace.

Her own anger started to burn like venom.

Thomas had arranged this. He had trapped them and led Hawkwood to death. If only there might be a moment to grab a sword and plunge it—

Without warning, the lead horse screamed.

Even as the first horse's scream died, there were yells of fear and the thud of falling bodies and then the screams of men.

Because of the hood over her head, Katherine's world became a jumble of dark confusion as her own horse stumbled slightly, then reared with panic. The sudden and unexpected motion threw Katherine downward to the ground at the side of the horse.

A roar of pounding hooves filled her eyes, and she felt something brush the side of her head.

The horses behind her! Would she be trampled?

Dust choked her gasp of alarm. More thunder of hooves, then a terrible crack of agony that seemed to explode her head into fragments of searing fire.

Then nothingness.

⚜

The light tickle of a butterfly woke Katherine as it settled on her nose. By the time she realized the identity of the intruder, it had already folded its wings shut.

Despite the deep throb in her head, Katherine suppressed a giggle. Her eyes watered from the effort of crossing them to focus on the butterfly, and even then, the butterfly was little more than a blur of color a scant inch away.

In any other situation, this would be a delight. *Such a gentle creature honors me with its visit.*

Her memory of the immediate past events returned slowly as the terrible throbbing lessened.

Hawkwood, dead. The procession of horses back toward York. Then a terrible confusion. Her fall. Unconsciousness. And now—

And now she could see. The hood no longer covered vision.

Katherine turned her head. Slowly. Not because of the resting butterfly on her nose. But because dizziness filled her stomach at the slight movement.

She discovered she was sitting. Rough bark pressed against her back. Her hands...her hands were free.

She brought them up, almost in amazement at the lack of pain biting tightly into her wrists. That movement was enough to startle the butterfly into graceful flight.

"The woman-child wakes," a voice said. "And with such prettiness, it is no surprise that even the butterflies seek her attention."

Katherine tensed. The voice belonged to a stranger behind her. Before she could draw her legs in to prepare to stand, he was in front of her, offering a hand to help her rise.

"M'lady," he said. "If you please."

If the man meant harm, he would have done it by now, she told herself. But what had occurred to bring her here in such confusion?

When she stood, aware of the rough calluses on the man's hand, she saw the aftermath of that confusion, beyond his shoulders, on the trail between the trees.

Two horses, unnaturally still, lay on their sides in the dust. Several others were tethered to the trunks of nearby trees. She counted four men, huddled at the edge of the trail. Their groans reached her clearly.

"It's really just an old trick," the man confessed modestly, snapping her attention back to him. "We yanked a rope tight across the bend. Knee-high to their horses. These fools were traveling in such a tight bunch and at such a speed that when the leaders fell, so did all the others, including you. I offer my apologies for the bandage across your head, but it was a risk we had to take. And we did not know you would be hooded."

Katherine gingerly touched her skull and found a strip of cloth bound just above her ears.

"It was not serious," the man said quickly. "The bandage is merely a precaution."

"Of course," Katherine murmured.

The man shrugged and grinned at her study of his features.

His eyes glinted good humor from beneath shaggy dark eyebrows. His nose was twisted slightly, as if it had been broken at least once, but it did not detract from a swarthy handsomeness, even with a puckered X-shaped scar on his right cheek. His smile, even and white, was proof he was still young, or had once been noble enough to enjoy a diet and personal hygiene that—unlike the diet and hygiene of the less fortunate—did not rot teeth before the owner had reached thirty years of age.

Indeed, traces of nobility still showed in his clothes. The ragged purple cape had once been exquisite, and his balance and posture were that of a confidence instilled by money and good breeding. His shoulders, however, were broad with muscles born of hard work, and the calluses on his hands had not come from a life of leisure. Altogether, an interesting man.

He interrupted her inspection.

"Your friend Hawkwood, I presume, escaped?"

His smile faltered as a spasm of grief crossed Katherine's face.

"That," he said gently, "is answer enough."

Katherine nodded. She was spared the embarrassment of showing a stranger unconcealed tears because of someone calling from behind them.

"Robin," a man cried. "Come hither."

He beckoned her to follow and turned to move to the voice. Together, they moved deeper into the trees and moments later entered a small clearing.

Katherine blinked in surprise. The remainder of the enemy's horses were gathered here. Isabelle sat on one, the two enemy knights on others, and Thomas on the fourth. Each was securely bound with ropes around their wrists. A dozen other men—not of the enemy group—stood in casual circles of two or three among the horses.

"Robin, it is high time we disappeared in the forest," the same voice said.

Katherine identified its owner as an extremely fat and half-bald man in a brown priest's robe.

"Yes, indeed," Robin replied. "The lady seems fit enough to travel." He paused. "Those by the road. They have the ransom note?"

The fat man nodded. "Soon enough they will find the energy to mount the horses we have left for them."

"They're lucky to be alive," spat another man. "I still say we should not bother with this nonsense about the lord's gold."

Robin laughed lightly. "Will, the rich serve us much better when alive." Robin motioned at Isabelle, who sat rigidly in her saddle. "The daughter alone is worth three years' wages."

Robin turned to Katherine.

"Yes," he said in a low voice. "We did promise to help Hawkwood by capturing Thomas. But we made no promise about neglecting profit, did we? And although the arrival of these men of York have complicated matters, there is now that much more to be gained by selling these hostages for ransom."

He lifted his eyebrows in a quizzical arch. "After all, as one of the most wanted of the king's branded outlaws, I can't be expected to be sinless."

TWENTY-EIGHT

Their southward march took them so deep into the forest that Katherine wondered how she might find her way back to any road.

The man she knew as Robin led the large but silent procession of outlaws and captives on paths almost invisible among the shadows cast by the towering trees.

It was a quiet journey, indeed almost peaceful. Sunlight filtered through the branches high above them and warmed their backs. The cheerful song of birds seemed to urge them onward.

Twice they crossed narrow rivers, neither deep enough to reach Katherine's feet as she sat secure on the horse Robin had provided. The men on foot had merely grinned and splashed through the water behind her. Katherine hoped each time that Thomas would topple from his own horse and flounder in the water with his hands bound as they were.

Never will that traitor be forgiven.

Again and again as they traveled, she reviewed the morning's horror. How had Thomas accomplished it? By prearranging his campsite so that the enemy knights knew exactly where to appear?

Again and again, she fired molten glances of hatred at Thomas's back. Of course Thomas had known the saddlebag had been leaking flour. To be followed so easily had made his task of flushing them out that much easier. How he must have chuckled as he waited for them in his camp.

Katherine needed to maintain the hatred. Without it to fill her, she would have to face the loss of Hawkwood. Without the hatred to consume her, she would have to focus on the struggle ahead. Yet even with the rage to distract her, questions still managed to trouble her.

With Thomas captured, what was she to do next? Without Hawkwood to guide her, what hopes had she of carrying on the battle against the Druids?

Each time those questions broke through her barrier of hatred, she moaned softly in pain and forced herself to stare hatred at Thomas's back.

It was after such a moan that the outlaw Robin halted the lead horse. He dismounted, then walked past all the others to reach Katherine.

"M'lady," he began, "we will leave all the horses here and move ahead on foot."

He answered the question without waiting for her to ask it. "A precaution. We near our final destination. The marks of horses' hooves are too easy to follow." Robin gestured to an outlaw. "Will shall lead the horses to safer grounds."

Katherine nodded, then accepted the hand that Robin offered to help her down from her horse.

"My apologies again," Robin said. "For you, as well as the others, must be blindfolded during the final part of our journey." His grin eased her alarm. "Another precaution. When the king's outlaws hide within the king's forests, it is only natural that we hesitate to show hostages—or visitors—to the paths to our camp."

Although none of the outlaws hesitated to call to one another across the camp, their voices were muted with caution.

It could have been the hush of the forest, however. The great trees in all directions blocked whatever wind there might be; the air in their shade was a blanket of stillness.

In the outlaws' camp, small campfires appeared in all directions as the shadows deepened with approaching dusk. At some, there was low singing of ballads. At others, the games of men at rest—arm wrestling, joke telling, and quiet laughter.

The fire at the center of the camp was much larger than any other. Beside it, turning the spit that held an entire deer over the flames, was the fat and half-bald man in a priest's robe. His face gleamed with sweat in the dancing firelight. In his free hand he held a jug of beer he replenished often from the cask beside him. A steady parade of men approached with jugs of their own for the same purpose.

Katherine leaned against the trunk of a tree and watched the proceedings with fascination.

How had Hawkwood known of these outlaws? How had he contacted them? And why had they agreed so readily to help?

At the thought of Hawkwood, her tears—now always so near—began to trickle again.

She blinked them away, then jumped slightly. The outlaw Robin had appeared in front of her in complete silence. *Surely in this darkness he cannot see my grief.*

"I would bid you join us in our eventide meal," he said. "I am told our venison will be ready soon."

"Certainly," Katherine replied in a steady voice. She did not feel any hunger.

"There is a message I have been requested to relay to you first, however," Robin told her.

Katherine waited.

"Thomas seeks a private audience with you."

The outlaw seemed to notice her posture become stiff.

"Do not fear, m'lady. He is securely bound. A guard is posted nearby."

Katherine noted with satisfaction that her tears had stopped immediately at the prospect of venting her hatred upon Thomas. "Please," she said, "lead me to him."

The outlaw took her to a small fire set a hundred yards away. As promised, a well-armed guard stood discreetly nearby.

"He is now yours," Robin said. Before departing, he added, loudly enough to make sure Thomas received the message, "And, m'lady, do not hesitate to call if he disturbs your peace. A sound whipping shall teach him manners."

Katherine nodded and the outlaw Robin slipped away with the same silent steps he had used to approach her.

She then turned to Thomas.

He sat on a log, hands bound in front, a chain around his waist and attached to the log. Nothing about his posture indicated captivity, however. His nose and chin were held high in pride.

"You requested my presence," Katherine stated coldly.

"Yes, m'lady," Thomas said in a mocking voice. "If it doesn't inconvenience you too much."

Katherine shrugged.

Thomas raised his bound hands and pointed at her, and his voice lost all pretense of anything but icy anger.

"I simply want to make you a sworn promise," he said in quiet rage.

"You seem in a poor position to make any promise," she answered with equally calm hatred.

"That will change," Thomas vowed. "And then I will seek revenge."

"Revenge?" she echoed.

"Revenge. To think that I almost believed you and the old man might be friends instead of Druids." He tried to stand, but the chain around his waist stopped him short. "The old man has already paid for his lies with death. And you, too, will someday regret the manner in which you betrayed my trust."

For a moment, Katherine could not get air from her lungs. She opened her mouth once, then twice, in efforts to speak. The shock of his audacity had robbed her of words.

"You…you…," she barely managed to sputter.

She looked about wildly and then saw a heavy stick in the nearby underbrush. Rage pushed her onward. She stooped to the stick, pulled it clear, and raised it above her head.

She advanced on Thomas.

He did not move.

"Barbaric fiend!" she hissed. "His life was worth ten of yours!"

She slammed the short pole downward. Thomas shifted sideways in a violent effort to escape, and the wood crashed into the log, missing him by scant inches.

It felt too good, the release of her pent anger.

She slammed the stick downward again. And again. Each blow slammed the log beside Thomas. He was no longer her target as she mindlessly directed her rage into the sensation of total release. Again and again she pounded downward.

A strange sound reached her through her exhaustion. She realized it was her own hoarse breathing and half-strangled cries of despair between gasps. She realized the heavy pole was now little more than a slivered pulp in her hands. And she realized Thomas stared at her in a mixture of fear and awe.

She poked the splintered pole at his face, and stopped it just short of his eyes.

"You craven animal—," she began, then whirled as the guard's hand gripped her shoulder while he spoke anxiously.

"M'lady—"

"This is none of your concern!" Her rage still boiled, and the guard stepped away in surprise.

She turned back to Thomas and jabbed the wood toward his face again. "How dare you slur Hawkwood's name! He was the finest Immortal of this generation! He was the last hope against you and the rest of the evil you carry! He was—"

Katherine had to stop to draw air. She wavered in sudden dizziness. Then as the last of her rage drained with her loss of energy, she began to cry soundlessly.

She had nothing left inside her but the grief of Hawkwood gone. After forcing back her sorrow for an entire day, she finally mourned Hawkwood's death. The tears coursed down her cheeks and landed softly at her feet.

Blindly, she turned away from Thomas.

His voice called to her. It contained doubt.

"An Immortal?" he asked quietly. "Why do you still insist on posing as a friend?"

"As your friend? Never." She could barely raise her voice above a whisper, yet her bitterness escaped clearly. "What you have betrayed by joining them is beyond your comprehension. Yet you Druids shall never find what you seek. Not through me."

"You Druids!" His voice began to rise again with rage. "I am exiled from Magnus. There is a bounty on my head! And you accuse me of belonging to those sorcerers?"

Katherine drew a lungful of breath to steady herself. "You knew we watched," she said. "Your masters sent you forth from York with Isabelle as bait for us."

"Sent me forth? Your brains have been addled by the fall. I risked my very life to take her hostage."

Katherine managed a snort. "Pray tell," she said with sarcasm. "How convenient, was it not, that the drawbridge remained open for you and not the pursuing knights? And explain how you managed to reach the puppet Earl of York inside the castle, even though he had been forewarned."

Thomas gaped. "Forewarned? You speak in circles."

Another snort. "Hardly. You pretend ignorance."

They stared at each other.

Finally Thomas leaned forward and asked in a low voice, "Who forewarned the earl, if not you, the people who managed to follow me when none other knew my plans?"

Had it been less dark, Thomas would have seen clearly the contempt blazing from Katherine's eyes. "I was a fool for you," she said. "Caring for you in the dungeon of Magnus when even then, your master Waleran was there. Then to discover him nearby in York..."

Thomas now gasped. "Waleran? In York? How did you know?" He stiffened in sudden anger. "Unless," he accused, "you are one of them. Leading those knights to my camp."

More moments of suspicious silence hung between them.

"Why?" Katherine then asked softly. "Why do you still pretend? And why did you betray us so? Is it not enough you were given the key to the secret of Magnus at birth?"

Thomas spoke very softly. "I pretend nothing. I betray no one. And this secret of Magnus haunts me greatly, more than you will ever know."

He continued in the same gentle, almost bewildered tones. "Katherine, if we fight the same battle, whoever betrayed us both would take much joy to see us divided." Thomas shook his head. "And if you are one of them, may God have mercy on your soul for this terrible game of deceit you play."

M'lady, what plans have you for the morrow?" Robin asked. Now, with dawn well upon them, lazy smoke curled upward from the dying fires.

Katherine huddled within her cloak against the chill of early day. She stood where she had remained motionless for the last four hours, staring at the embers of the campfire nearest her.

"M'lady?"

With effort, Katherine pulled herself from her thoughts and directed her gaze at Robin.

"Plans? I cannot see beyond today."

Robin gently took her elbow and guided her to the main campfire where the fat outlaw, still with a jug of beer in his free hand, now stirred a wooden paddle in a large iron pot.

"Broth," Robin directed the fat man. "She needs broth."

With catlike grace and surprising nimbleness for such a large man, a bowl was brought forth and filled to the brim from the pot.

Robin helped Katherine lift the bowl to her mouth. When she tried to set it down after a tiny sip, he forced it back to her mouth again. And again. Until finally, enough warm, salty soup had trickled down her throat to make her realize that she was famished.

Greedily, she gulped the soup, then held it out for more.

Robin smiled in satisfaction. He waited until she had finished two more bowls before leading her to a quiet clearing away from camp.

"Tell me now," he said, "what plans have you for the morrow?"

Katherine stood straighter now, and much of her wild hopelessness had disappeared.

"None." She smiled wanly. "Not yet."

"I have discovered," Robin said slowly, "that to make plans, one must first decide one's goal. Then it is merely a matter of finding the easiest path to that goal."

Despite herself, Katherine chuckled. "Knowing the goal, my friend, presents little difficulty. The path to that goal?" She shrugged. "One might as well plan a path across open sky."

The outlaw shrugged. "The task is not that impossible. After all, birds fly."

"They are not armed with weapons to destroy."

"M'lady, what is it you want?"

Katherine thought of the secrets she had shared so long with Hawkwood. Sadly, she said, "I cannot say."

The outlaw studied her face, then said quietly, "So be it. But if I, or my men, can be of service…"

Katherine, in return, studied the older man's face, almost as if seeing it for the first time. "Why is it," she asked, "that you offer so much? First to rescue me and capture Thomas. And now this?"

"Hawkwood never told you?"

Katherine shook her head.

"We had been captured once," the outlaw said. He rubbed the scar on his cheek. "Captured and branded like slaves. Held in the dungeons of Scarborough. The rats and fleas our only companions. The night before our execution, all the guards fell asleep…"

Robin's face reflected wonderment. "Each guard was asleep like a baby, and suddenly Hawkwood appeared among them. One by one, he unlocked our doors and set us free. When he got word to us to arrange your capture, we were glad to pay our debt."

Katherine hid her smile. Child's play for one of the Immortals. A tasteless sleeping potion in food or wine. It did not surprise her that Hawkwood might release innocent men or that he would know how to reach them later. His foresight had almost been perfect—had not the knights of York appeared, he and Katherine could have pretended surprise at the outlaws' appearance and lulled Thomas into revealing more.

"When?" Katherine asked. "When did this happen?"

"Some years ago," the outlaw replied. "We learned our lesson well. Since then, the sheriff's men have not seen so much as a hint of us." He grinned. "Except, of course, through the complaints of those we rob."

He went on quickly at Katherine's frown. "Only those corrupted by power," Robin explained. "Those who will never face justice because they control the laws of the land."

"You will continue to be a thorn in the sides of those who reign now, the Priests of the Holy Grail?"

"It will be our delight to provide such service."

A new thought began to grow in Katherine's mind. She spoke aloud. "My duty," she said, "is to fight them also. No matter how hopeless my cause might seem, I must strive against them."

Robin nodded. No doubt he understood well the nobility of effort.

"I have little chance to succeed," Katherine continued. "But what chance there is, I must grasp it with both hands."

"Yes?" Robin sensed she had a request.

"Offer to battle Thomas. Set the stakes high. His life to be forfeit if he loses or his freedom if he wins."

"M'lady?"

Katherine spoke strongly, more sure each passing second of what she must do in the next weeks. "Then," she said, "make certain that you lose the battle."

"As you wish," he said, "or my name isn't Robin Hood."

THIRTY

ENGLISH CHANNEL, LATE SPRING—AD 1313

M'lady?"

Isabelle ignored the voice behind her. She knew it belonged to the sailor that she'd sent on an errand. He'd delivered the information that she had needed. His body odor was horrible enough to be noticed, cutting through all the other odors of the docks, from fish guts to spoiled food to the smell of urine at the corner of every alley.

"M'lady?" His voice was louder, more insistent.

She finally turned, within the shadows of the overhang of a building on the street. Beyond, she could see a glint of water of River Hull, which opened here to the channel between England and the mainland. It was good to be free again, but this was not a moment to think of the circumstances that had led her here. Instead, she had an important matter at hand.

"My business with you is finished," she said, finally turning to face her follower.

Indeed it was. Isabelle had followed Thomas here and had felt fortunate not to lose him when he disappeared for far too long between the outlaws and this port, where he had boarded a ship on the docks of this town, Kingston upon Hull. King's Town upon the River Hull. Twenty years earlier—around the time that her father Lord Mewburn had taken Magnus—King Edward and a hunting party had chased a hare that led them to the banks of the River Hull. The King had not only been charmed by the beauty of the scene of waters and hills, but had realized the potential of the site for shipping. He'd purchased the land from the Abbott of Meaux, issued proclamations to encourage development, and given it the royal name, King's Town.

It was rapidly becoming the foremost port on the east coast, prospering by the shipping of wool and woolen cloth, and importing wine. The shipping destinations were so diverse that Isabelle had had to hire this sailor to report back to her about the destination of the ship on which Thomas had paid for passage. It could have been headed to Scotland in the north, across the channel to Holland or France, or as far south as Spain.

When the sailor had returned with the information that Thomas was going to Lisbon in Portugal, she'd considered her money well spent, especially after the sailor found her another ship with the same destination, leaving a few days earlier than Thomas's. She would be waiting for Thomas when he arrived, able to finally learn what he intended by fleeing England.

"I know you have no further business with me," the sailor said, nodding and bowing. He smiled, showing pride in his single tooth. "Yet there is another who sent me to request a meeting with you. The man you inquired about on the ship that goes to Lisbon the day after next."

Thomas. She should have known he would have found out about her. It seemed always that he was a couple of steps ahead. For all she knew, Thomas had only made it appear that the Priests of the Holy Grail had conquered Magnus, and this was simply another part of his game.

"Where is he?" she asked.

"Follow," the sailor said, pointing down a street.

With the ever-present gulls swooping and squawking above, Isabelle remained a few paces behind, but the wind was blowing the wrong direction, and even at that distance, the man's odor was as repellent as his appearance.

Thomas.

She was alone here, trusted by those who sent her to complete her task.

Alone. There would be nothing to stop her from betraying those who sent her. And their cause. She had half-decided that she would do it, if only Thomas would agree to flee from them with her. He had gold. She had gold. They could board a ship together. Find a place safe from Druids. And both of them could leave the battle and live in peace. It was dream that she'd first forced away from her thoughts, then allowed to return again and again, so that it almost seemed real.

Thomas.

Thinking of him, she lost her customary caution and turned into the alley behind the sailor. He stepped into a doorway, and when she followed, he sprang out again, holding a knife low, its blade pointed upward. The expert move of a man accustomed to a street fight, a man prepared to sweep the point of the blade into a man's belly. Or, like now, her belly.

"Into the doorway," he ordered, motioning with the knife.

She did as commanded.

"Your gold first," he said, standing so close that his breath washed over with a stench of sewage. "If you scream, you'll only have time to scream once, and it will be lost among the gulls. It will be your last scream, and I'll have the gold anyway."

"My gold?"

"Don't play innocent with me. I know you have plenty of gold. You've paid me, and you've paid to secure passage to Lisbon. You may be wearing clothing of a peasant, but your skin is too fine and your body too nourished to be a commoner."

He grinned widely, showing gums again and the single tooth. "And a commoner would not be stupid enough to follow a sailor into an alley. You're about to discover why a woman like you should never travel alone.

The gold is in a pouch hanging from your neck. Safe from pickpockets, perhaps, but not from me."

Isabelle reached to her neck and pulled out the pouch.

Keeping his knife at the ready, he reached out with his other hand. She reached across, and as he took it, she raked her nails across the top of his hand.

He grunted with pain and stared at the scratches that welled with blood.

"That will cost you," he said. "I had been intending to kill you quickly, but now there will be nothing gentle about it. And I'll make sure I enjoy it."

Isabelle forced herself to look into the filth of the man's face. Both the filth of grime and the filth of his leer.

"Think about your hand," she said, "and ask yourself if anything about it feels strange."

He waved his knife at her. "No tricks. It won't gain your freedom."

"There's no trick at all," she said. "But you will notice I have a second pouch around my neck."

She pulled at the cord and lifted out the pouch, leaving the cord around her neck. She shook the pouch to indicate there was no jangle of gold coin. "And your hand. A strange sensation? Burning?"

The sailor frowned. He shook the hand that she'd scratched.

"Ah," she said. She held out her own hand. "You'll notice I'm very careful never to touch my eyes or mouth."

The sailor's frown turned into a grimace, and he shook his hand harder, as if a dog were attached to it. "What madness is this?"

"Not madness, but a fast-drying poison from a foreign land where soldiers there use it to coat the tips of their arrows. All it takes is a scratch from the arrow, and the person dies within minutes. Those soldiers have arrows, but I prefer to coat my own nails with it."

She smiled. "This pouch contains pills to counteract the poison. I keep the pouch with me as protection, should I ever accidentally scratch myself."

"Open the pouch," he grunted, threatening her with the knife. "Now."

Isabelle spilled the contents of the pouch onto her palm, showing small tablets of compressed herbs and powders of various sizes and colors.

"You'll see your guts spilled on the dirt if you don't give me the pill by a count of three."

"You can count that high?"

"One…" He grunted again with pain, and terror crossed his face.

"The burning," she asked, "it's climbing your arm?"

"Two…" He was frantic, and she feared he would thrust the knife in his panic.

Isabelle daintily plucked a small pill from her palm and handed it to the sailor. He popped it into his mouth and forced it down with an audible swallow.

Isabelle cupped her hand and poured the remainder of the pills back into the pouch. She tightened the top of the pouch with the cord and dropped it below her neck again, out of sight in her clothing.

She watched the sailor with a smile on her face.

His own expression was a puzzled frown. It didn't last long. His eyes rolled back in his head, and he sagged to his knees.

"I had wondered what that pill would do," she told him, not even sure if he could hear anymore. But, of course, she knew exactly what it would accomplish. No Druid reached her age without a comprehensive knowledge of herbs and roots, and every Druid held such a pouch to cover a wide range of contingencies.

She sighed. "I suppose it's obvious, isn't it, that I gave you the wrong one."

On his back now and crumpled in a contorted fashion, he could not answer.

She stepped over him, and, breathing through her mouth to avoid his stench, plucked her gold pouch from his open hand.

She took a step away, then spun around and grabbed his knife.

The sailor had definitely been correct about one thing. It was dangerous for a woman to travel alone.

She kept the knife.

THIRTY-ONE

I've already said it once. Board this vessel alone, or not at all."

Thomas, in reply, merely shifted the puppy beneath his arm to the other. It was a deliberate act, done slowly to show he had no fear of the loud sailor. It was also a difficult act. The cloak Thomas wore did not encourage his movement. Yet he would not ever consider traveling without the cloak. Thomas understood well why Hawkwood had worn such a garment. It concealed much of what he must always carry hidden upon him.

The sailor facing him jabbed a dirty finger in the air to make his point. "A dog and all its fleas. We're not interested in having a beast wander around underfoot, tripping one of us and sending a man overboard. Or dropping filth for one of us to step upon. Hah! Might you be thinking this is Noah's Ark?"

The sailors around him, always eager to watch a confrontation, laughed loudly.

"Aargh! Noah's Ark! Good one, Cap'n!" The laughter continued in waves as that joke was passed from crewman to crewman.

Thomas had secured passage upon the *Dragon's Eye*, a merchant ship, one that was already near full with bales of wool from the sheep that grazed on the hills of the inland moors. It was one of the few merchant ships not owned by the Flemings or Italians. That he had been able to barter his passage in English had been a blessing; facing the jeers of the sailors was a small price to pay.

As he stared at the sailor, silence finally settled upon them, broken only by the constant screaming of gulls as they dipped and swooped for the choicest pieces of garbage on the swells of the gray water beside them.

"This creature once saved my life," Thomas said calmly, "and you will receive the full price of passage for him."

The sailor squinted. "Eh? You'll pay double just to keep the mongrel beside you across the North Sea and down the Atlantic?"

Thomas nodded. Around him, the stench of rotten fish, of their entrails discarded carelessly in the water, of salt-crusted damp wood forever soaked with fish blood, and of mildewed nets.

Now he looked directly into the sailor's eyes, bloodshot and bleary above a matted beard.

"Double passage," Thomas repeated firmly. To prove his point, he quickly produced another piece of gold.

The sailor in front of him coughed politely.

"Well, we welcome you aboard. You and your companion." The sailor smiled, but there was no kindness in his eyes. "It would appear you both deserve to be treated like kings."

⚜

A deck hand led Thomas to the rear of the *Dragon's Eye* and chattered like a man who was far too accustomed to lonely weeks at sea with a crew of only eighteen, none with anything new to discuss.

"You picked a fine ship, you did," the deck hand said. "A cog like this handles the roughest seas."

The cog was over one hundred feet long, with a deep and wide hull to hold the bulkiest of cargoes. Thomas stepped around the bales of wool. Above him, the single sail was furled around the thick, high center mast.

Thomas had seen cogs leaving the harbor with open sails and knew it was large enough to drive the boat steadily in front of any wind.

"It's not fast, nor an easy boat to maneuver," the deck hand continued, like one eager to impart knowledge, "but it's almost impossible to capsize."

He lowered his voice. "And its high sides make it difficult to be boarded at sea by pirates."

He smiled at the result he had hoped to achieve. Thomas's face had darkened with sudden concern.

"Look about you," the deck hand waved. "The castle at the prow"—his voice became smug—"the fighting tower at the front is how I should explain it proper for you land people, lets us fire arrows and such from above at any raiders who draw close."

He then waved at their destination on the cog, ahead of them by some fifty feet and several dozen tons of wool piled in orderly stacks of bales. "The sterncastle—the tower at the rear—is for important guests."

The deck hand sighed. "A bed and privacy. What gold can't buy!"

Then he remembered he had superiority because of his knowledge and immediately began lecturing again. "We've got oars—we call them sweeps—should the gales be too rough or should we need to outrun pirates. You might be asked to man one then."

Now, Thomas said or did nothing to stop the flow of words he barely heard.

Dangerous gales and pirate attacks. What folly had brought him here? The words of an old man who had betrayed him. And some vague references in his secret books. Such madness to begin the journey, let alone hope in its success.

Yet what else was there to do? The reward on his head had been increased, and with the Priests of the Holy Grail slowly controlling town after town, there soon would be no place safe left for him in northern England. Unless he chose to live the uncertain life of an outlaw, and his contest for life and freedom against that wily Robin Hood had shown how dangerous that might be.

The deck hand interrupted his thoughts. "Here you are. The sterncastle. My advice is that you tie the dog inside. There'll be enough grumbles about a dog enjoying the shelter denied us crew without his presence outside as a daily reminder."

Thomas nodded.

The deck hand hesitated, an indication he knew he should not ask. But his curiosity was too strong. "Our destination is Lisbon. Do you intend to go beyond Portugal?"

The scowl he received from Thomas was answer enough.

I'm fortunate we depart before you hear about the gold offered for my head. The less you know the better.

The deck hand stumbled back awkwardly to make room for Thomas to enter the dank and dark sterncastle.

Most certainly the Druid spies will someday discover I escaped England on the Dragon's Eye, *and eager will be the sailors to impart that information for the slightest amount of gold. They cannot know my destination is that of the Last Crusaders. Jerusalem. The Holy City.*

THIRTY-TWO

If the deck hand believes this to be luxury, Thomas thought with a sour grin, *then he and all the crew have my sympathy.*

As if in agreement at the squalor of the dark and cramped quarters, hardly more than walls and a low roof, the puppy beneath his arm whined.

"You like it no more than I?"

Thomas set Beast on the rough wooden floor. He shivered, then crawled beneath the crude bed.

"They told us two weeks to Lisbon if the weather is favorable," Thomas told his now-unseen companion. "And crossed themselves when I asked how long if the weather wasn't."

Another answering whine.

Thomas smiled. A week earlier, Beast had first growled fearlessly as Thomas entered the cave after his absence of several days, caused, of course, by the time spent captive among the outlaws led by Robin Hood. The fearless growls had then changed to yips of total joy as the puppy had recognized Thomas.

Thomas had responded to the barking and jumping with equal joy, something that had surprised him greatly. True, he had not intended to leave the dog to die slowly in the cave, and indeed, he had worried upon his capture that the puppy would die the slow lingering death of starvation. But Thomas did not want to be burdened with concern for anything except his goal of winning Magnus. And, until that joy at their reunion had so surprised him, he had intended to leave the puppy somewhere with peasants. Instead, he had spent two days in the cave, poring through the ancient pages of knowledge or staring in thought at the natural rock chimney that allowed sunlight to enter, uncaring of the aches that still battered his every move because of the fierce fight with Robin Hood.

Those two days he had puzzled his next move. Yes, Magnus seemed out of reach. But almost before he had learned to run, the quest for Magnus had been instilled in him by his mother, who disguised herself as his childhood nurse.

Without Magnus to pursue, what else had he in life?

So, despite the near impossibility of his task, he could not let it go.

And at the end of the second day in the cave, Thomas realized the only chance of victory, no matter how slim, would be in trusting Gervaise one more time and uncovering the reason the books had been hidden. The only clues he had were vague references to the Last Crusade, written in the page margins of two of the books. And simply because they were too similar to what was in the book given him by Hawkwood during their midnight discussion before the betrayal, he had realized he could not ignore what it meant.

A sudden wave nearly pitched him against the far wall of his quarters. He recovered his balance, but realized the wave was a brutal reminder of the obstacles ahead. Had he chosen correctly the direction for his search? Or was the old man's book merely bait? To be wrong meant a year wasted, one more year for the Priests of the Holy Grail to add strength to their hold over the area around Magnus.

"*Strive to do your best here on earth,*" Thomas heard the patient voice echo in his mind, "*yet in all your pursuit, remember and take heart that it is only the first step toward something much greater.*"

At that thought, Thomas's eyes watered. Gentle and kind Gervaise, the calm speaker of that lesson, now too, like his mother, Sarah, had surely passed from this life, and all in effort for Thomas to save Magnus.

God rest their souls. Thomas finished his prayer with a sudden determination to continue his quest, if only because of the sacrifices others had made. *And God be here on these cold gray waters with mine.*

Thomas opened his eyes. He had little hope of returning to England, let alone any victory over the Druids who held Magnus.

THIRTY-THREE

Shortly after dawn on the third morning, Thomas wanted to die.

"Carry your own bucket out," the sailor snarled into Thomas's cramped quarters. Thomas sat hunched over his knees on the edge of his bed. "We've no time for soft-headed fools around here."

The sailor half-dropped and half-threw the empty bucket in Thomas's direction, then slammed the door in departure.

Thomas could not even lift his head to protest.

A small part of his mind realized that the deck hand had been right about bringing Beast aboard. For two days, food had been brought to his quarters. For two days, each visitor bearing that food—except for a small, dirty cook's assistant who had stooped to let the puppy lick his hands—had grumbled about wasting it and valuable space on a useless dog.

The larger part of his mind, however, thought nothing about Beast or the obvious resentment among the crew.

Thomas truly wanted to die.

The cog, as promised by the first deck hand, rode the rough seas with no more danger of sinking than if it had been a cork. However, like a cork, it tossed and bobbed on top of the long swells of water as the winds slowly took the cog south through the English Channel and into the vast North Atlantic Ocean.

Only once had Thomas been able to stagger to the door of his quarters to look out upon those waves, green-gray and hardly any different in color than the bleak sky. The waves had seemed like small mountains, bearing down on the vessel without mercy, lifting it high, then throwing it down again, only to be repeated by the next rushing surge of tons of water.

That sight had propelled him back into the quarters again, where he had fallen to his knees and emptied what little remained of the contents of his stomach into a bucket there for that purpose.

It did not help that the food offered with such little grace consisted of biscuits, salted herring, and weak mead. Merely the smell of the food within the bucket was often enough to make Thomas heave again into the smaller bucket, also meant to serve as a portable latrine.

Beast seemed oblivious to the sea. Indeed, he seemed to delight in the pitches and rolls of the ship, and bounded around the small quarters with enthusiasm.

"Traitor," Thomas muttered to the puppy as he now attacked the food. "Is it no wonder you grow like a weed, taking my portion with such greed."

The puppy did not bother to look up.

A vicious wave slammed the side of the cog and knocked Thomas a foot sideways.

He groaned at the nausea that overwhelmed him and prepared for the now-familiar tightening and release of his stomach. His ribs racked with renewed pain as he leaned over the slop bucket and violently threw up.

⚜

The cold wind bit the skin of his face and throat and provided Thomas a slight measure of relief as he lurched from his quarters at the rear of the ship.

Below him, in the belly midship, was the crude tentlike roof of cloth that sheltered the crew from the wind and inevitable rain. Men moved in and out of the shelter, all intent on their various duties.

Thomas carried the slop bucket to the side of the ship and braced his legs to empty it over the side. He was so weak that it took all his energy and concentration to keep his balance and not follow the contents overboard.

He turned back to retrace the few steps to his quarters. And nearly stumbled into the large sailor who blocked his path.

"By the beard of old Neptune," the sailor said with a nasty grin, "you would favor us all by becoming food for the fish."

Thomas saw something cold in the man's eyes, and beyond the man's shoulder, he noticed two other sailors entering his quarters in his absence. He understood the implications immediately.

"I had feared pirates at sea," Thomas said. He had to swallow twice to find the strength to continue and was angry at the weakness it showed so clearly. "But I did not expect them aboard this vessel."

The sailor leaned forward, his eyes yellow above a dirty beard. "Pirates? Hardly. We saw the color of your gold and know the ship's captain charged too little by far for us to bear the insult of living so poorly while a dog lives so well."

Thomas sucked in lungs full of cold air, hoping to draw from it a clearness that would rid him of his nausea.

"Rate of passage is the captain's realm," he finally said.

The sailor took Thomas's hesitation as fear, and laughed. "Not when the captain sleeps off a night's worth of wine!"

There was a loud yelp from the quarters, then a muffled curse. The other two sailors backed out. One held his hand in pain. The other held the puppy by the scruff of his neck.

"No signs of coin anywhere," the sailor with the puppy said. He dangled the puppy carelessly and ignored its yelps of pain.

The other sailor grimaced and squeezed his bleeding hand. "That monster took a fair chunk from my thumb."

The yellow-eyed sailor turned back to Thomas. He dropped his hand to his belt and, with a blur of movement, pulled free a short dagger.

He grinned black teeth.

"Consider your choices, lad. 'Tis certain you carry the gold. You'll hand it over now. Or lose a goodly portion of your neck."

Thomas knew the sailor was lying—once they had the gold, he would die anyway. Alive, he would later be able to complain to the captain, or once ashore, seek a local magistrate. The sure solution for them was to make sure no one was watching this far corner of the ship, and toss him—alive or dead—overboard. Then, no one aboard would be able to prove the crime.

Show weakness, Thomas commanded himself. *Your only chance against three is to lull them into expecting no fight at all.*

He sagged, an easy task considering the illness that seemed to bring his stomach to his throat.

"I beg of you," Thomas cried, "spare my life! You shall receive all I have!"

The evil grin of blackened teeth widened.

"Of course we'll spare your life," the yellow-eyed sailor promised. He jabbed his knife forward. "Your coin!"

All three laughed at how quickly Thomas cowered in reaction to the movement of the knife.

Then Thomas fumbled with his cloak. "I keep it in a pouch hanging from my neck," he said, not needing much effort to place an extra quaver in his voice. "'Twill take but a moment."

Long before—it now seemed like a lifetime—Thomas learned something about swordplay in the dungeon cells of Magnus with Sir William. The knight had shown him the design of a leather sheath that was strapped around his upper body, so that a sword might remain hidden high on his back, between his shoulder blades. The knight had shown him the art of drawing the sword quickly, a Roman short sword capable of deadly work in close quarters. Later, when both were free from the danger and away from prying eyes, the knight had made Thomas practice the move again and again.

"Reach for your neck, as if scratching a flea," the knight had said, *"then in one motion, lean forward, draw it loose, and slash outward at your enemy."*

"T-the knot is a-awkward," Thomas explained in a stammering voice as he fumbled with his right hand at his throat. He bent forward slightly, as if reaching behind his neck for a knotted string of leather. "But it will only take—"

He did not finish.

The hours of training had not been wasted.

In one silk-smooth move, the sword drew free over his ducked head. Head still down, he struck at the spot he had memorized before bending—the knife hand of the yellow-eyed sailor.

A solid *thunk* and squeal of pain rewarded him, even as he raised his head to give him a clear view of all three.

The sailor's knife bounced off the wood deck.

Without pause, Thomas kicked the yellow-eyed sailor, sinking his foot solidly into the man's groin. Then, even as the man fell forward in agony, Thomas charged ahead, slashing sideways and cutting steel into the flesh of the second sailor's shoulder.

The third sailor only managed to step back half a pace, but even in that time had brought his arm back to cast the puppy overboard.

He froze suddenly.

"I think not," Thomas grunted.

The sailor did not disagree. He slowly lowered the puppy, careful not to move in any way that might encourage Thomas to press the point of the sword any harder into the hollow of his throat.

"Let the puppy fall," Thomas said softly. "He'll find his feet. Or you might not find your head."

The sailor could not even nod, so firmly was the sword lodged against his flesh. He simply opened his hand. The puppy landed softly, then growled and bit the sailor's ankle. Tears of pain ran down the man's face, but no sound could leave his throat.

"Obey carefully. This sword may slip," Thomas warned. "My balance on these pitched waves has proven difficult."

The sailor's eyes widened in agreement.

Thomas pointed left with his free hand, and the sailor slowly shuffled in that direction. Thomas kept the sword in place and shuffled right, and in that manner of a grotesque dance, they continued until Thomas had half-circled and now faced the other two wounded sailors.

Beast stood directly between his legs and growled upward at all three sailors. "Listen to him well," Thomas said. All three sailors bled soundlessly. The yellow-eyed one with the bones showing on the back of his hand. The second one with a gash through sleeve and shoulder. And the third from a torn ankle.

"Listen to my friend well," Thomas repeated. "The next time your greed will cost you your lives."

Even as the next words left his mouth, however, Thomas knew by the hatred from their eyes that they would return. A colder, more ruthless man would understand this and kill them to eliminate a future threat. Tossing their bodies overboard would solve his problem—no one on the ship, save Beast, had witnessed the fight. It would be assumed the men had simply fallen overboard.

Thomas tried to will himself to slash out with the sharp steel. Saving his own life would be that simple. But he could not. He was helpless, for he would have to betray every instinct he held to kill them now in cold blood.

He allowed them to stumble away, and even then, one of them turned and mumbled a curse.

Thomas scooped up Beast and returned to his quarters.

THIRTY-FOUR

Thomas could only guess the time when he next left his quarters, for low and angry gray skies hid the sun's location.

He grinned upward despite the bleakness of the forbidding sky and endless swells of water. Dizziness and nausea had finally left him. After days without food, after days of constant vomiting, he was famished.

He carried the empty food bucket and swayed in rhythm to the motion of the ship as he walked to the edge of the rear deck. From there, he slowly studied the movements of the crew below.

Nothing seemed threatening.

For a moment, he considered seeking the ship's captain to set forth his accusations against the three.

Then he dismissed the idea. Whose side would the captain chose? Certainly not his. With a crew of eighteen men, the captain would never risk becoming the focus of all anger by trying to discipline one-sixth of the crew.

No, Thomas could only hope that he had shown enough willingness to fight that the crewmen would not feel it worth the effort to cause more trouble.

Yet there was the sailor with the yellow eyes.

Thomas felt the man would return. And probably when all advantages were his. It would be a long, long journey, Thomas told himself, even if the cog were to reach Lisbon in the next hour. And there were many days ahead.

A slow, small movement below demanded his attention and tore him from his thoughts.

Yet, as he had been taught, Thomas refrained from glancing immediately at its source. No, by yawning and stretching and swiveling his head as if he had a sore neck, he was able to direct his gaze at the movement without showing any interest.

Only the cook's assistant. Hat over eyes, shifting in sleep in a corner away from the constant menial work of preparing food.

Thomas looked elsewhere. Only briefly. The weight of the empty bucket was an unnecessary reminder of his intense hunger.

Thomas whistled, low and sharp.

He sleeps soundly.

Thomas whistled again. This time, the cook's assistant raised his head and opened bleary eyes.

Thomas waved for him to approach the short ladder that led up to his quarters from the main deck of the cog.

"I beg forgiveness for waking you," Thomas began, for he could remember his own days of back-grinding labor and little rest. "But I grow faint with hunger."

Thomas lifted his empty bucket and smiled. "You could earn yourself a friend."

The cook's assistant shrugged, face lost in shadows beneath the edge of the battered leather cap, and took the offered bucket. When he returned, Thomas climbed down the ladder, reached into the bucket and used his teeth to tear apart a hard biscuit. He swallowed water from a jug in great gulps and then filled his mouth with the salted herring.

Thomas ate frantically in silence, half-grinning in apology between bites. When Thomas finally finished, he wiped his mouth clean with the sleeve of his cloak.

"You have my gratitude," Thomas stated with good-natured fervor.

Once again, the cook's assistant shrugged, then held out his hand for the bucket.

"A moment, please," Thomas asked. "Have you any news of three crewmen in foul tempers?"

Raised eyebrows greeted that question. *What face I can see is so dirty,* Thomas thought, *hair so filthy, he is fortunate it is cut too short to support many fleas. And his clothes are hardly more than layers and layers of rags.*

"Of course," Thomas said, laughing at the silent response to his question. "All sailors have foul tempers."

A guarded smile greeted his joke.

"Three men," Thomas prompted, "with wounds in need of care. Has any gossip regarding their plans reached your ears?"

Another shrug. Then the cook's assistant touched his forefinger to his own lips.

Thomas understood. Mute.

The cook's assistant set the bucket down and cupped his hands together, palms upward. He then stroked with one hand the air above the other.

"Puppy?" Thomas asked. "You inquire as to its well-being?"

The cook's assistant nodded, almost sadly.

"His belly is fat with the food I could not eat." Thomas smiled lazily, happy to be seasick no longer. "At least only one of us needed to suffer."

The cook's assistant opened his hands wide.

"Why?" Thomas interpreted. "Why so much trouble for a worthless puppy?"

He answered his own question. "That creature saved my life. It is the only living thing I dare trust."

Then, speaking more to himself than to his audience, Thomas said very softly, "And it is the only living thing that trusts me in return."

THIRTY-FIVE

They attacked when the moon was at its highest.

The clouds had broken early evening, some six hours earlier, and the water had calmed shortly after. The dark of night provided peace to the weary crew. While the constant creaking of the ship continued, no longer did it groan and strain with every wave.

Thomas saw every move of their advance.

Crouched low, and silent with stealth, they slipped from bale to bale until reaching the ladder.

There were only three.

Thomas could enjoy the observation of their deadly approach because he was far from his quarters, hidden in the shadows of bales of wool. Far too easy, should the opportunity arise, for an unwary sleeper to be trapped inside those quarters, and far too easy for a knife of revenge to be drawn across his throat. So he had chosen the discomfort of the open ship.

Seek what treasures you will, Thomas thought merrily. *Seek it until dawn. For what you desire rests safely with me.*

Within his cloak lay his gold. Warm against his side lay the puppy, squirming occasionally with dreams.

I shall rest during the day, Thomas silently promised the three sailors, *and spend my nights at constant guard among these shadows.*

Much to his satisfaction, angry whispers reached Thomas. There was a light bang of the door shutting and a grunt of pain. More angry whispers.

Then silence. Minutes of silence.

It began to stretch Thomas's nerves, knowing they were above him,

out of sight, about to appear in silhouette at the top of the ladder at any
moment.

Thomas wanted the warning, wanted to know as soon as possible when
they were about to descend. But he did not stare at the top of the ladder.

Instead, he chose to focus on a point beyond it. Night vision, he knew,
caught movement much more efficiently at the sides of the eyes.

Silence continued. Now the creaking of the ship seemed to be the low,
haunting cries of spirits.

Suddenly, Thomas's heart leaped in the terror of shock.

Directly above him, the edge of the deck detached itself!

He managed not to flinch, then forced himself to be calm, and slowly,
very slowly, turned his head to see more clearly.

The black edge of the deck had redefined itself to show the black out-
lines of a man's head and shoulders.

*These men are shrewd. They have decided I must be hidden nearby. Instead
of choosing the obvious—the ladder—they now watch from above, hoping I
will not notice and betray myself with a movement.*

Thomas told himself he was safe as long as he remained still. After all,
he had chosen a deep shadow.

Yet his heart continued to hammer at a frantic pace. *This is what the
rabbit fears, hidden among the grass. I understand now the urge to bolt before
the hounds.*

But Thomas did not.

Instead, what betrayed him was the only creature he trusted.

The puppy, deep in dreams, yelped and squirmed.

And within seconds, two of the sailors dropped to the belly of the ship.
One from each side of the upper deck.

Beast yelped again, and they moved with unerring accuracy to the bale
that hid him.

Moonlight glinted from extended sabers.

Thomas barely had time to stand and draw his own sword before they were upon him.

"A shout for help will do no good," came the snarl with the approach of the first. "The captain's drunk again, and the crew have turned a blind eye."

"For certain," a harsh whisper followed. "None take kindly to the manner in which you crippled my hand."

Thomas said nothing, only waited with his sword in front.

Beast, now fully awake, pressed against his leg and growled at the attackers.

Another movement as the third sailor, the one with the limp, scuttled down the ladder from the upper deck. He, too, brandished a saber.

I have been well trained, thought Thomas, *by Robert of Uleran, the man who surely fell in my defense at Magnus. I shall not disappoint his memory by now falling myself without a worthy fight.*

The sailors circled Thomas, shuffling slowly in the luxury of anticipation. The silver light of the moon made it an eerie dance.

Impossible to watch all three at once.

From which direction would the first blow come?

Thomas heard the whistle of steel slicing air, and instinctively stepped back. He felt a slight pull against the sleeve of his cloak, then—it seemed like an eternity of waiting later—a bright slash of pain and the wetness of blood against his arm.

"Ho, ho," the yellow-eyed sailor said, laughing. "My weaker hand finds revenge for the damage you did the other!"

The sailors circled more.

One dodged in and dodged back, daring Thomas to attack, daring Thomas to leave the bale behind him and expose his back.

The others laughed in low tones.

This is the game. Cats with a cornered mouse. They are in no hurry.

"Gold and your life," the second sailor whispered. "But only after you beg to be spared."

The other two chortled agreement.

Until that moment, Thomas had felt the deep cold of fear. His blood would soak the rough wood at his feet; that he knew. But their taunts filled him with a building anger, and his fear became distant.

"Beg?" Thomas said in a voice he hardly recognized as his. "Should I die, you will die with me. This is a fight that will cost you dearly."

The yellow-eyed sailor mimicked his voice with a high-pitched giggle. "This is a fight that will cost you dearly."

That slow-growing anger suddenly overwhelmed Thomas. He became quiet with a fury that could barely be restrained.

He lifted his sword and pointed it directly at the yellow-eyed sailor and spoke with compressed rage. "You shall be the first to taste doom."

The yellow-eyed sailor slapped his neck. Then, incredibly, as Thomas lowered his sword to a protective stance, the yellow-eyed sailor sank to his knees, then soundlessly fell face forward onto the deck.

What madness is this?

Thomas had no time to wonder. The second sailor betrayed a movement, and Thomas whirled to face him. Still carried by that consuming rage, Thomas pointed his sword at the man's eyes.

The man grunted with pain, eyes wide and gleaming with surprise in the moonlight. He, too, dropped to his knees and tumbled forward to land as heavily as a sack of fish.

What madness is this?

Thomas answered his own bewilderment. *Whatever it might be, this is not the time to question.*

He spun on the third sailor, who now staggered back in fear.

Thomas raised his sword and advanced.

"No!" the man shrieked loudly in terror. "Not me!"

Then he gasped, as if slapped hard across the face. His mouth gaped open, then shut before he pitched forward.

That shriek had pierced the night air, and from behind Thomas came the sounds of men moving through the ship.

He gathered his cloak about him, scooped Beast into his other arm, and fled toward the ladder.

THIRTY-SIX

Thomas had fourteen nights and fifteen days to contemplate the miracle that had saved his life, fourteen nights and fifteen days of solitude to puzzle the events. For not a single member of the crew dared disturb him.

The three sailors had risen the next day from stupor, unable to explain to the crew members who had dragged them away what evil had befallen them at the command of Thomas's sword.

Each day, the cook's assistant had been sent with food. Each day, the cook's assistant had darted away without even daring to look Thomas in the eye.

While fourteen nights and fifteen days was enough time for the shallow slice on his arm to heal, it was not enough time for Thomas to make sense those scant minutes of rage beneath the moonlight.

Many times, indeed, he had taken his sword and pointed it at objects around him, disbelieving that it might have an effect, but half-expecting the object to fall or move, so complete was his inability to understand how he, in his rage, had been able to fell three sailors intent on his death, without touching one.

And for fourteen nights and fifteen days, he fought the strange sensation that he should know what had happened. That somewhere deep in his memory, there was a vital clue in those strange events.

On the sixteenth day, he remembered. Like a blast of snow-filled air, it struck him with a force that froze him midway through a troubled pace.

No, it cannot be!

Thomas strained to recall words that had been spoken to him in near panic the night Magnus fell to the Priests of the Holy Grail.

He had been hidden in a stable, saved from death only because of his guise as a beggar, while the castle fell.

As Thomas projected his mind backward, the smells and sounds returned as if he were there again. The pungent warmth of horses and hay, the stamping of restless hooves, the blanket of darkness, a tired, frightened old woman clutching his arm, and the messenger in front of him.

"M'lord," Tiny John had blurted, *"the priests appeared within the castle as if from the very walls! Like hordes of rats. They—"*

"Robert of Uleran," Thomas had interrupted with a leaden voice. He wanted to sit beside the old woman and, along with her, moan in low tones. *"How did he die?"*

"Die?"

"You informed me that he spoke his last words."

"Last words to me, m'lord. Guards were falling in all directions, slapping themselves as they fell! The priests claimed it was the hand of God and called for all to lay down their arms. It was then that Robert of Uleran pushed this puppy into my arms and told me to flee, told me to give you warning so that you'd not return to the castle..."

No, it cannot be, Thomas repeated as he remembered. Yet the Druids had posed as those false Priests of the Holy Grail; the Druids had mysteriously appeared within the castle—undoubtedly through the secret passages, which only in his last hours there had Thomas discovered riddled Magnus—and the Druids had somehow struck down the well-armed soldiers within.

Guards were falling in all directions, slapping themselves as they fell.

Yellow-eye had slapped himself, then fallen.

A Druid was aboard this same ship.

Thomas had little time to search or wonder. An hour later, a shout reached him from the sailor on watch at the top of the mast.

The port of Lisbon had been sighted.

THIRTY-SEVEN

T*o present myself as bait would be difficult under any circumstance,* thought Thomas. *But to be bait without knowing the predator, and to be bait in a strange town with no idea where to spring and set the trap is sheer lunacy.*

Especially if that strange town is a danger in itself.

Lisbon sat at the mouth of the wide and slow River Tagus, a river deep enough to bring the ships in and out of the harbor area. The town itself was nestled between the river and two chains of hills rising on each side. It was one of the greatest shipping centers of Europe, for the Portuguese were some of the best sailors in the world.

Thomas stood at the end of a crowded street that led to the great docks of Lisbon. He leaned from one foot to the other, hoping to give an appearance of the uncertainty that he truly felt.

Which eyes follow me now?

Impossible to decide.

Hundreds upon hundreds, perhaps thousands of people flooded the docks of Lisbon. Swaggering men of the sea, cackling hags, merchants pompously wrapped in fine silk, soldiers, bellowing fish sellers.

Sea gulls screamed and swooped. Wild and vicious cats, fat from fish offal, slunk from shadow to shadow. Rats, bold and large, scurried up or down the thick ropes that tethered ships to shore.

It was confusion driven by a single purpose. Greed. Those canny enough to survive the chaos—human or animal—also thrived in the chaos. Those who couldn't were often found in the forgotten corners of alleys and never received a proper burial.

Thomas knew he needed to find such an alley, if only to finally expose his follower. And he only had a few hours of sunlight left. For he knew he would need the protection of a legion of angels should he be foolish enough to wander these corners of hell in the dark.

He moved forward, glad once again for the comfort of the puppy beneath his arm.

⚜

It took half of the remaining daylight to find the proper place for ambush.

He had glanced behind him occasionally, only during the moments he pretended to examine a merchant's wares. Spices from Africa once, exquisite pottery from Rome another time, and strange objects of glass called spectacles, which the bulky man with the too-wide smile had assured him were the latest rage among highbred men and ladies all across Europe.

Not once had Thomas spotted a pursuer during those quick backward glances. Yet he dared not hope that meant he was alone or safe. Not after the strangeness of men collapsing because of an upraised sword.

Then, during his wanderings, he had noticed a side alley leading away from the busy street. He walked through once and discovered it opened, after much twisting and turning, onto another busy street. The alley itself held many hidden doorways, already darkened by the shadows of late afternoon.

So Thomas circled, an action that cost him much of his precious time. In the maze of streets, it was no easy task to find the original entrance to the alley again.

Once inside that tiny corridor between ancient stone houses, Thomas smiled. Here, away from the bustle of the rest of the town, it was almost quiet. And, as with the first time through, it was empty of any passersby. He could safely assume any person who traveled through it behind him was his follower.

Thomas rounded a corner and slipped into a doorway.

He set Beast down, fumbled through his travel pouch for a piece of dried meat, then set that on the cobblestone.

"Chew on that, you little monster," Thomas whispered. "I have no need for your untimely interference again."

Beast sat on his hindquarters and happily attacked the dried meat in silence.

Will it be flight or fight? Thomas wondered. His heart hammered against his ribs as each second passed. He knew he was well hidden in the shadows of the doorway. He could choose to let the follower move on and in turn stalk the stalker, or he could step out and challenge his unknown pursuer. Which would it be?

More seconds passed, each measured by several rapid beats of his heart. Beast remained silent.

Thomas did not hear footsteps. Rather, his pursuer moved along the cobblestone so quietly that only his long shadow stretching out before him hinted at his arrival.

When the figure appeared in sight, head and neck straining ahead to see Thomas, the decision came instantly.

Fight.

For the figure was barely the size of a boy.

Thomas reached out and grasped for the shoulder of the small figure. His reaction was so quick that Thomas only managed a handful of cloth as that figure spun away and sprinted forward.

But not before Thomas recognized the filthy face and hat.

The cook's assistant.

Thomas bolted from the doorway in pursuit.

The cook's assistant? Surely he is a mere messenger or spy. Yet his capture is my only link to his masters.

Thomas ignored the pain of his feet slamming against the hard and irregular cobblestone. He ducked and twisted through the corners of the tiny alley, gaining rapidly on the figure in front.

Behind Thomas came the frantic barking of the puppy as he joined in this wonderful game.

Thomas closed in, now near enough to hear the heaving of breath ahead.

Three steps. Two steps. A single step away. Now tackle!

Thomas dove and wrapped his arms around the cook's assistant. Together, they tumbled in a ball of arms and legs.

Get atop! Grasp those wrists! Don't let him reach for a dagger!

Thomas fought and scrambled, surprised at the wild strength of this smaller figure. For a moment, he managed to sit squarely on his opponent's stomach. A convulsive buck threw him off, and Thomas landed dazed.

The cook's assistant scuttled sideways, but Thomas managed to roll over and reach around his waist and pull him back close into his body.

Then Thomas froze.

This is not what I should expect from a cook's assistant. Not a yielding softness of body that is more like…

Angry words from this mute cook's assistant interrupted his amazement and confirmed his suspicion.

…more like that of a woman.

"Unhand me, you murderous traitor."

It was the voice of Katherine.

Thomas scrambled to his feet and grabbed her wrist to help her upward.

She slapped his hand away and reached her feet with a grace that made Thomas feel awkward.

Even without the hat that had always cast shade over her face aboard the ship, those layers of dirt and that filthy hair cropped short still made it difficult to recognize her, yet it truly was Katherine.

She glared hatred at him and spat on the ground beside him.

Yes, it is she indeed.

The puppy skidded to a halt between them.

Thomas barely noticed.

"You...what...how?"

He did not finish his stammered sentence.

Katherine looked over his shoulder and her eyes widened.

There was a slight rustle and the sound of rushing air. Then a terrible black pain against his skull overwhelmed him.

When he woke, it only took several seconds to realize he was in a crude jail. Alone.

THIRTY-EIGHT

T homas groaned aloud. He touched the back of his head—a foolish move, for he already knew how badly it ached, and his gentle probing of a large lump brought renewed stabs of pain.

Early-evening light filtered through a tiny square hole hewn through the stone.

The dimming light showed a straw-littered floor, stone walls worn smooth with time, so confining that he could touch all four easily from the center of the cell.

Thomas stood, and groaned again.

He felt an incredible thirst and staggered to the door. He thumped it weakly.

What evil has befallen me now?

As he waited for a response, he puzzled over this turn of events. *Who has thrown me here? Why? Did that devil's child Katherine have others to help?*

There was no answer, so Thomas thumped the door again. The impact of the heel of his hand against wood worsened the throbbing of his head.

My cloak. My gold. The old man's book. My sword and sheath. Gone.

It finally dawned on Thomas that he had been stripped down to his undergarments.

In anger, he pounded the door again.

"Release me," he croaked through a parched throat. "Return my belongings."

Faint footsteps outside the door reached him as the echoes of his words faded in the twilight of his cell.

Then, a slight scraping of wood against wood as someone outside slid
back the cover of a small partition high in the door.

"Your majesty," a cackling voice called in sarcastic English heavily ac-
cented with thickened Portuguese vowels. "Come closer."

Thomas did.

"Do you stand before the door?" that voice queried. "Beneath the
window?"

Thomas looked directly above him at the hole in the door, which permitted the voice to float clearly through.

"Yes," Thomas answered.

"Good. Here's something to shut your mouth for the night."

Without warning, a cascade of filthy water arched through the opening. Drenched thoroughly, Thomas could only sputter.

"And I've got buckets more if that doesn't instruct you on manners.
Now let me sleep."

The partition slammed shut, and footsteps outside retreated.

Thomas moved back to the side of his cell and gathered straw around
him. Already he was beginning to shiver.

Shortly after the first star appeared in the small, square patch of sky that
Thomas could see from his huddled position, across his feet ran the first rat
of many in a long, sleepless night.

⚜

"Your majesty has a visitor." That heavy Portuguese accent interrupted
Thomas's dreams.

Thomas opened gritty eyes to look upward at the face of a wrinkled
gnome. A toothless grin leered down at him.

"Why should you enjoy sleep?" the voice continued.

Thomas began to focus, and the ancient gnome became an old tiny man with blackened gums that smacked and slobbered each word. "If I'm to be wakened this early, so must you."

The gnomelike man pointed back over his shoulder at the open doorway. "Why a common thief like you would receive such a visitor is beyond any mortal's understanding."

Thomas ignored the man. And ignored the constant throbbing of his head, the itching of straw and flea bites, and the thirst that squeezed his throat.

He was transfixed by his visitor.

Katherine.

Not the Katherine he had seen in any form before. Not the Katherine as a noble friend, disguised as a freak in the wrapping of bandages. Not as the Katherine whose long blond hair had flowed in the moonlight during her visits as a midnight messenger. Not the Katherine who had betrayed him first to the Druids, then the outlaws. Not the Katherine covered with grime as a cook's assistant.

Thomas gaped at the transformation.

Gone was the filth. Gone were the rags.

Instead, a long cape of fine silk almost reached her feet. Holding the cloak in place was an oval clasp, showing a sword engraved into fine metal. Her neck and wrists glittered with exquisite jewelry. Her hair—still short— had been trimmed and altered to highlight the delicate curves of her cheekbones.

She would put a queen to shame.

Thomas fought against the surge of warmth that struck him at that mysterious and aloof smile.

She is one of them, he warned himself, *one of the Druids who have taken Magnus.*

He opened his mouth to speak, and she shook her head slightly to caution him against it.

"This most certainly is my runaway servant," she said sternly. "I shall see he is whipped thoroughly."

Servant?

The gnomelike man nodded with understanding. "Feed them and clothe them and still they show no gratitude."

Servant?

"I have spoken to the authorities," Katherine continued. "The boy that this"—Katherine sniffed scorn and pointed at Thomas—"scoundrel attacked has not reappeared to seek compensation. Given that, and the fortune in gold that changed from my hands to the magistrate's, I have been granted permission for his return."

The gnomelike man somehow shook his head in sympathy. "Is he worth this?"

"A promise to his mother, a longtime servant," Katherine answered. "She was dear to our family, and we vowed never to let her son stray."

"Ah," the jailer said.

He kicked Thomas. "Be sure we don't see your face again."

Thomas pushed himself to his feet. His back felt like a board from leaning against the cold stone, his legs ached from shivering, and his head still throbbed. Now he was to be treated as her servant?

Yet what were his alternatives? He shuffled forward meekly. *Wait,* he promised himself, *until she and I are away from listening ears.*

Not until the jailer retrieved Thomas's outer garments did he realize how immodest it was to be standing there in his undergarments. He seethed with frustration as he dressed, stumbling awkwardly as he balanced from one leg to the next under her gaze.

Then Thomas followed her through the narrow corridor, not daring to wonder what poor souls wasted away behind the other silent wooden prison doors, into the bright sunlight outside.

They stood at the north end of the harbor, and the noise and the confusion of the chaos of men busy among ships reached them clearly.

"Where is Beast?" Thomas asked.

"Beast?"

"The puppy."

"Your first question is about a dog?"

"Answer it." Thomas didn't care how surly he appeared.

"Fear not," Katherine said sweetly. "As the cook's assistant, I spirited away your puppy. It remains safely waiting for you at the inn."

"Take me there, then, and after, I shall be on my way."

"And where is that?" she asked with a smile.

Thomas groaned at his headache. "Away from you."

"I think not. You were arrested yesterday," Katherine reminded him, "as you lay there gasping like a stunned fish."

Thomas rubbed the back of his head. "What foul luck. Certainly a harbor such as this has only a handful of men who guard and patrol for the townspeople."

"He was pleased to be such a hero," Katherine said. "Rarely do such bold crimes occur in broad daylight. He also seemed pleased at the accuracy of his blow."

She paused. "It cost fully a quarter of your gold to pay your ransom."

"My gold?" Thomas sputtered.

"Of course," Katherine said calmly. "I lifted your pouch as I helped them drag you away."

"You used my gold?"

"Had I not, the jailer certainly would have. After all, did he not keep your sword and sheath?"

Thomas ground his teeth in anger.

"And my remaining gold?" Thomas spat each word.

Her voice remained sweet. "Much of it purchased this fine clothing. I needed to pose as a noblewoman retrieving an errant servant. Besides, it would serve neither of us for me to remain as a mere deck hand on our next voyage."

"Much of it? Next voyage?" He caught the implications. "*Our* next voyage?"

"I hardly think this was your final destination."

"I travel alone," Thomas declared.

"Not unless you jump ship," Katherine said smugly. "I need only say the word and you will be thrown in jail again. Until we leave Lisbon, you are mine, and under my orders you will board the ship of my choice."

"You have much to explain." Thomas dared not trust himself to say more. His fists were clenched in fury.

"Perhaps. But as my penniless servant, you are in no position to dictate any terms."

She favored him with another radiant smile.

"And my first command is that you bathe. You smell wretched."

THIRTY-NINE

Y ou should find the servants' quarters somewhere below," Katherine said as they stepped onto the gangway.

Thomas gritted his teeth. Katherine had been shrewd enough to dispense an amount of gold that would guarantee eternal loyalty from the port authorities.

Twice, in fact, he had rebelled during this long day since his release from prison. Was it not bad enough she had refused to return to him his remaining gold? Was it not bad enough she had taken such enjoyment at his discomfort—before and after his time in the public bath? Twice he had stormed from her, uncaring that he was penniless in a strange town. And twice he had been overtaken by a pair of guards who offered him the alternative of jail or a return to his master, that wonderful noblewoman.

So now he stood on the gangway that led to the galley *Santa Magdellen*, an Italian merchant galley. This ship, unlike the *Dragon's Eye*'s single mast with square sail, had two masts with lateens—triangular sails—which, in the calmer seas of the Atlantic and Mediterranean, enabled the ship to sail into winds with a minimum of tacking back and forth.

Thomas scowled at Katherine. But discreetly. He could see lurking behind her on the dock the two guards and remembered they had not been gentle in the manner in which they had persuaded him both times earlier to return to her instead of jail.

She smiled back. Sweetly, of course.

He wanted to stitch her lips together, anything to rid her of that assured smile. He wanted to shake her by the shoulders and loosen the words from her mouth, words to explain how she had followed him and how she had known his destination, to find passage on a galley that sailed to Israel, the Holy Land. And—far worse—he wanted to be able to stare into those taunting blue eyes for every heartbeat for the rest of his life.

That confusion only served to deepen his foul mood.

She is one of them, he forced himself to remember each time their eyes met. *I should not feel this insane warmth.*

So he growled surly agreement at her directions to the servants' area and began to march to the cramped and foul area of the ship that would be his home for several weeks.

"Thomas!" she called before he took three steps.

He turned around and scowled again.

She pointed to the expensive leather bags at her feet, which held her considerable array of travel possessions—all purchased with his gold. One of the bags held the smuggled puppy. Neither wanted trouble with this crew.

"Must you forget the simplest of duties?" Katherine asked. "Surely you don't expect me to carry these bags to my quarters."

⁂

It took nearly an hour to leave the harbor. The galley was awkward at slow speeds, and the ship's captain dared not raise the sails until they reached the open sea.

The crew used oars instead; Thomas was half-surprised that Katherine had not volunteered his services as an oarsman.

In the hum of activity of departure, Thomas easily moved unnoticed to the prow of the ship where Katherine stood and enjoyed the breeze above the water.

Spray cascaded against the wooden bow as the galley rose and fell with the waves. That sound made it easy for him to approach her back without being heard.

"Have I not been tortured enough?" he asked. He was tall enough that he had to bend to speak the words into her ear.

She turned and stepped back, not startled—or refusing to show surprise—at his sudden presence. "I've hardly begun," she said. "But this is a long voyage, and I remember well your treatment of me as I hung upside down by a rope."

"Do not hold those foolish dreams of revenge," Thomas said. "We are away from those wretched Lisbon watchdogs. I shall be my own man now."

She smiled. "If you glance over your shoulder, you will see unfriendly eyes closely watching your every move."

Thomas groaned. "Not so."

"Indeed," Katherine informed him. "Your gold has proven to work wonders with the ship's captain as well. He has promised to have you whipped, should you exhibit the same behavior that jailed you in Lisbon."

"My gold cannot last for eternity," Thomas protested. "Silks, perfumes, rich food, passage, and now protection! I had planned to live for a year on that gold."

"Wool," Katherine said.

"Wool?" Thomas stared at her as if she had lost her sanity.

"Silks, perfumes, rich food, passage, protection. And wool."

"Wool?" The despair of comprehension began to fill his voice.

"Wool," she repeated patiently. "This merchant ship holds twenty tons of wool that I purchased with your gold. Even after the price of passage, I should profit handsomely with its sale when we arrive in the Holy Land."

"Impossible," Thomas said through lips thinned with frustration.

"Oh no," Katherine assured him. "Wool is much needed in far ports."

"I meant impossible that I had enough gold for twenty tons of wool." Thomas could hardly speak now, so difficult was it to remain in control.

Katherine dismissed that with a cheerful wave. "Had I neglected to inform you that I borrowed heavily from the supply of gold you have hidden in England?"

His mouth dropped.

"Remember?" she prompted. "Near the cave that contains your secret books?"

A strangled gasp left his throat. Thomas clutched his chest.

"It was child's play to follow you to Kingston upon Hull after your contest with the outlaw Robin Hood. All I needed to do was return to that cave and wait for your arrival."

She lifted an eyebrow and pretended surprise. "You expected that I would remain with the outlaws to share the ransom collected for Isabelle?"

Thomas closed his eyes briefly, as if fighting a spasm of pain.

"Thomas, Thomas," she chided. "Surely you don't believe it was your doing to win the contest with the outlaw?"

His eyes now widened.

"Robin Hood had been instructed to lose. I wanted you set free."

She moved closer to him and mockingly placed a consoling hand on his arm. "Take comfort, however. He admitted later the outcome was not certain, even had he wanted to defeat you."

Thomas slapped her hand away.

"Woman," he said fiercely, "you have pushed me too far."

He grew cold with rage as he continued. "My fight for Magnus was a deathbed promise to my mother. Every pain suffered to fulfill that pledge is a pain I would gladly have suffered ten times over."

He stepped closer—now controlled in anger—but did not raise his voice.

"Yet even after victory, the strange secrets behind Magnus haunted me. And each new secret glimpsed has had your face. I fight enemies I cannot see, and I fight enemies I wish I could not see. Too many good men have sacrificed themselves for this fight."

He advanced while she backed to the railing.

"Yet the reason for this fight—a reason I am certain you know—has been kept from me. And even the reason it has been kept from me has been kept from me."

He paused for breath. "Your face and those secrets follow me here to the ends of the earth. And now I am your prisoner on a tiny ship in vast waters. You have stolen my gold. You have humiliated me."

He raised his forefinger and held it beneath her chin. "And now you mock me in tone and words. I will take no more."

Thomas stepped back and said in a whisper, "From this moment on, wherever you stand on this boat, I will choose the point farthest away from you. Threaten me, punish me, have me thrown overboard. I do not care. For I wash my hands of you."

He stared at her for a long moment, then let scorn fill his face before turning away.

She called to his back immediately.

"Forgive me," Katherine said. The mocking banter in her voice had disappeared. "Love leads one to do strange things."

He turned.

"Que je ne peux pas vous aimer," Katherine said.

Thomas was still stunned by her first words. So it took his befuddled brain a moment to translate. "Would that I could not love you," she had just said. Why French?

"And I have loved you fiercely since I was a child," she was now saying. Although he understood those words clearly, it took Thomas another moment to realize her last sentence had been spoken in faultless German.

Loved him since she was a child?

"I see by the light in your eyes," Katherine said, now in English, "that you understand well my words. And that is part of why I cannot not love you."

"Truth and answers," Thomas replied, using Latin. "Only a fool would throw away love offered by you, but first I need truth and answers."

She smiled at his switch in language and answered him in Latin.

"Can you not now see we have received the same education? Have we not been driven mercilessly by our teachers to be literate and fluent in all the civilized languages when few in this world can even read in their own tongue?"

She moved to Thomas again and placed her hand on his forearm. This touch, however, was tender, not mocking. "And have we not been trained to fight the same fight against the same enemies?"

She looked beyond Thomas and discreetly removed her hand from his arm. Hawkwood had given her permission to extend some trust. "The ship's captain approaches. Tonight, let us talk."

FORTY

The five hours until moonlight seemed to take as long as the entire voyage from England to Lisbon.

Thomas had stood on the stern platform, staring at the coastline directly eastward that became little more than a faint haze with distance. Beast pressed against his leg, content to have his company.

I dare not trust her, he had told himself again and again. *Her vow of love is merely a trick. For if she were not one of them, how else could I have been captured in my camp the morning after her arrival with the old man?*

Yet the old man had spoken of the Immortals, raised from birth to fight the evil spawned by generations of a secret society of Druids. *I had almost believed him—until my capture through their betrayal proved they were Druids posing as Immortals.*

And yet, too, I must consider the alternative. If Katherine is an Immortal and can truly explain the apparent betrayal, she is my only hope to recapture Magnus, my only source to the secrets that have plagued me. If she is Druid, I will play the game to find what she really wants. So I must pretend to believe her. And refuse to let my heart be fooled as it so desperately wants.

Thomas remained on the stern platform all those hours until she appeared.

Her hair was now silver in the moonlight, her face a haunting mixture of shadows.

I cannot read her eyes. How do I dare trust her words?

"You know by now that a secret war rages," she began without a greeting. "Druids, who have chosen darkness and secrecy as the way to power, contend with the Immortals, who battle back in equal secrecy."

Thomas nodded.

"You and I were born to Immortal parents," Katherine said. "But not even birth destines a child to be an Immortal. Some, in fact, live and grow old unaware of their parents' mission."

Thomas held up a hand to interrupt.

"Certainly I know of the Druids," he said. "Their circle of evil is ancient. The Roman emperor Julius Caesar observed them more than twelve hundred years ago, when they still reigned openly in Britain."

Katherine nodded. "Of course. You know that from your books in the cave. But of Immortals—"

"Of Immortals, I know nothing more than their name, as mentioned by my nurse, by Hawkwood, and by another I knew in Magnus. It is more than passing strange that once I heard the Immortals referenced to Merlin—the same name of King Arthur's wise man and trusted counselor."

"More than passing strange," Katherine agreed. "King Arthur and his knights ruled some hundreds of years after the Roman conquerors had taken Britain and forced the Druids into hiding openly."

"Hiding openly?"

"Openly. The safest way to hide. Blacksmiths, tanners, farmers, noblemen, knights, priests during the day. But at night..." Katherine's voice trailed. "At night they would meet to continue their quest for power."

She shivered although the night air was warm. "Frightening, is it not? Any man or woman you might meet in England—a dark sorcerer at night. And many strove for positions of power in open society, the better to influence the direction of their secret plans."

Thomas spat disgust, but said nothing. He knew too well the treachery of Druids.

"Merlin?" he prompted her.

"Yes. Merlin. Eight hundred years ago. The brightest and best of the Druids."

Thomas stood transfixed. The creaking of the ship, the passing of water, the clouds slipping past the moon—he was aware of none of it.

"Merlin was a Druid?" he asked.

"It explains much, does it not? His powers have become legendary. Some call him an enchanter. Equipped with the knowledge of a Druid— knowledge that is considerable and often seems magic to poor, ignorant peasants—he accomplished much through deception. And what better place for a Druid than at the right hand of Britain's finest king?"

Thomas shook his head, trying to understand. "Yet he battled…"

"Yet Merlin battled the same Druids who raised him to such power. Merlin founded generations of the Druids' greatest enemies, each person equipped with the knowledge of a Druid. In short, he turned their own powerful sword upon themselves."

"Why?" Thomas asked softly. He let his mind drift back those eight hundred years to the court of King Arthur. Sir Galahad, Sir Lancelot, and the other Knights of the Round Table. And Merlin, the man who established that Round Table, at the right hand of Britain's most powerful man. "Merlin had everything a man might desire. Why risk losing all by rejecting the same Druids who had given him that power?"

"It is legend among us," Katherine said equally softly. "The Druids had waited generations for one of them to have the power in open society that Merlin did. With Merlin, finally, there was one to set into motion the plan that would let them conquer the entire kingdom, a plan so evil that its success would establish the Druids forever. Merlin was the one man able to ensure success. Until he became the one man to stop them. The legend is that a simple priest showed Merlin the power of faith in God by—"

"A bold plan to establish the Druids?" Thomas interrupted. "It failed with Merlin. Is it the plan they follow now that Magnus has been conquered?"

"Yes," Katherine said quietly. "Merlin stopped them once. And established the Immortals. Us. And since then, we have fought them—generation by generation—at every turn. We have held them at bay. Until they finally discovered where we had hidden ourselves."

"What is at the end of this evil plan?" Thomas asked.

Hesitation. Then Katherine said, "I do not know. He always promised to tell me. But he never had that chance."

Does she lie? Or are her faltering words because of grief for the old man?

Thomas paced back and forth several times, then asked, "The Immortals also hide openly?"

"Yes."

"And seek positions of power to counteract the influence of Druids?"

"Yes." Katherine smiled. "Sometimes we reach fame through these efforts. And we reach far. Generations ago, Charles the Great, king of the Franks, sent for educated people from all over Christendom. He wanted his people to learn again, from books."

Katherine paused, trying to recall the story. "The Druids had arranged to send one of their own there. What better way to spread evil in other countries? We intercepted the orders and replaced that Druid with a man named Alcuin. He rose quickly within the royal court of the Franks and did untold good, spreading knowledge and even introducing a new style of writing."

She waved her hand. "There are others, of course, through the ages. We have all been taught the stories of our history."

Thomas frowned. "How many of us are there?"

Katherine sighed. "Before Magnus fell twenty years ago, hundreds.

More than enough to keep the Druids from reaching their goal."

"And now?"

"I...I...do not know. I have only the stories that taught me."

She became quiet, as if the memory of the old man was too hard to bear.

Thomas sensed her sadness and tried to occupy her with other thoughts. "Hundreds? How could hundreds be taught in secrecy? That would take hundreds of teachers!"

"Not so," Katherine replied, her voice not entirely free of sorrow. "Merlin devised a new method. He appointed his successor before he died. And each successor appointed another, so that Merlin's command was passed directly from generation to generation of the Immortals. Each leader was the finest among us and selected teachers who, in each generation, shared knowledge with entire groups who sat together. One teacher had as many as thirty listeners."

Thomas whistled appreciation. "'Tis wondrous strange. Yet seems so simple. Now it strikes me odd that this method is not followed elsewhere."

Katherine nodded. "Merlin called it 'school.'"

Thomas stumbled over the strange word. "School."

Much now made sense.

Magnus. Isolated in the moors north of England, far from the intrigues and attention of reigning monarchs.

Magnus. With only moderate wealth, not a prize worth seeking.

Magnus. Insignificant, nearly invisible.

Magnus. The largest fortress in the north, a construction that must have cost a king's ransom, far more than the land itself could earn even with the profit of centuries of income.

Magnus. Seemingly with nothing to protect.

Magnus. Riddled with secret passageways.

Thomas understood.

He stopped pacing abruptly and voiced his certainty to Katherine.

"Merlin established Magnus. Obscure and well protected, it has been the training ground for every generation that followed."

"Yes," she said. "Merlin chose Magnus and had the fortress built. He retired to the island in that remote land. From there, he taught the Immortals and sent them throughout the country to combat the Druids in hidden warfare. And Magnus served us well for hundreds of years. Even after the Druids finally discovered its location and purpose, it took generations for them to conquer it. I was not there when that happened, of course, but Hawkwood told me that their surprise attack and ruthless slaughter twenty years ago all but destroyed the Immortals. Only a few survived."

She stopped, and in the dim light, Thomas could see she was trying to search his face.

"And Thomas," she finally whispered, "shortly after his birth, a boy was chosen as Merlin's successor of this generation to reconquer Magnus for us. That child...was *you*."

FORTY-ONE

Thomas stood and squarely faced her, with feet braced and arms crossed. It was the only way he could stop the trembling that threatened to overwhelm him.

I want so badly to believe her.

"You weave a fanciful tale," he said scornfully. "Yet if it were true, why was I not told of this?"

"But you were, in a way," Katherine said softly. "Was it an accident you were hidden in that obscure abbey? Was it an accident that your mother, Sarah, gladly exiled herself there to raise and train you as thoroughly as if you had been raised in Magnus as son of the reigning earl?"

That startled Thomas into dropping his bluff of indifference.

"Sarah had been commanded to keep the truth from you. Your father, the ruler of Magnus, was the appointed leader of his generation of Immortals. It was too important that no one ever discover your real identity, and it was feared that as a child, you might blurt it aloud before the wrong ears."

Thomas shook his head. "Sarah would have told me everything about Druids and Immortals, if it were so."

Katherine disagreed, sadly. "No. As I once explained to you, many of the Immortals fell with Magnus. Hawkwood often told me you were our only hope, that should the Druids discover the only son of the last leader of the Immortals was still alive, they would leave no stone in England unturned in their search to have you murdered."

Thomas raised his hands helplessly. "I should have been trusted. I stumbled in the darkness." His voice became accusing. "Alone."

Katherine put a finger to her own lips to silence his protests. "When Sarah died, you were too young to be trusted yet with that precious knowledge. And there was no one who could replace her at the abbey to instruct you more. Hawkwood often told me we could only trust that her training had been a magnificent seed, that you would learn more from the books left with you, and that you would always remember Magnus."

Thomas shook his head again, more firmly. "Yet I ruled Magnus for three seasons. Neither you, nor Hawkwood, nor Gervaise revealed this to me then."

Katherine moved to the edge of the ship and stared away. Thomas was forced to follow to be able to listen to her words before they were swallowed by the breeze.

"We could not," she said, still staring at the moon. "For you had been alone at the abbey far too long. We could not know if the Druids had found you and claimed you as one of their own."

"I conquered Magnus! I took it from them!"

Katherine sighed. "Yes. I argued that often with Hawkwood. He told me that we played a terrible game of chess against unseen masters. He told me they might have artfully arranged a simple deception, that the more it seemed you were against them, the more likely we might be to tell you the final truth, and in so doing lose this centuries-old battle in the quickest of heartbeats."

Thomas pondered her words and spoke slowly. "What is the final truth?"

The constant splash of water against the side of the galley was his only reply.

"The final truth," he demanded.

"Not even I was told."

She lies. I can sense that, even with her face turned away from me. Yet I must pretend to believe.

So Thomas said, "There is an undeniable logic in that. How could you ever believe that I was not a Druid, posing as one of you? So I was watched. By Gervaise, who posed as a simple old caretaker. And by you, in your disguise beneath the bandages."

"I am relieved you understand."

There is a simple flaw with this entire story. And it breaks my heart. Yet I cannot leave it lie.

So Thomas spun her to face him and squeezed both her wrists without mercy.

"But explain," he said fiercely, "why you finally tell me this now. And explain it well, for otherwise I believe nothing. Otherwise I shall cast you overboard."

"No, Thomas," she begged. "You must let go!"

His response was to pull her closer to the edge of the ship. She must believe this terrible bluff. "Speak now—," Thomas began, but he had no chance to continue.

Her eyes widened and she called out, "No!"

But her cry was not directed at Thomas.

He heard a scuffling of feet and began to turn his head. Late, much too late. A familiar blackness crashed down upon him.

⚜

Thomas dreamed that gigantic court jesters juggled him as if he were a tiny ball, laughing and yelling as they tossed him back and forth.

He woke with a muffled shout just as the most hideous jester dropped him, and discovered indeed he had been tossed back and forth, but in the confines of the brig in the belly of the ship.

Thomas propped out a hand to keep from pitching back to the other side and waited for his eyes to adjust to the dimness. The extent of his new prison—walls of rough wood and iron bars for a door—made the cell in Lisbon seem like a castle.

His head felt as if it might split.

Uncanny, he thought with a twisted grin, *they managed to hit me in the exact spot of my previous lump. Do bumps grow atop bumps?*

He was able to contemplate this imprisonment for several hours before he had a visitor.

"No," he groaned at the scent of perfume, "curse me with your presence no longer."

"Hush," Katherine said. "I risk too much even now. A real noblewoman saved from the attack of a rebellious servant would never grace him with a visit."

Thomas shook his head slightly, but at the reverberations of pain, held it very still. "You had us watched as we spoke," he accused. "And they believed I would harm you."

"Would you?" Katherine asked.

"Then, no." He touched the back of his head. "Now, yes."

She smiled. "I have little time. Yet I want to answer your question."

Thomas studied her face through the iron bars.

"In Kingston upon Hull," Katherine began, "you made an error. You sought advice from an old hag who sold fish, advice on how to reach the Holy Land."

Thomas shrugged, then winced. "Unfamiliar with the ways of the sea, I needed that advice. And I dared not ask any ship captain. I did not want him to know my destination. So I asked her, thinking she would never remember a passing stranger."

"A passing stranger with a tail sticking out of his cloak as he walked away."

"Beast." He lurched upward. "Where is—"

"Now safely hidden in my quarters," Katherine assured him. "From the old woman, I discovered your destination. There was only one ship in the harbor leaving for Lisbon. It was not difficult to sign on as a cook's assistant."

"Why—"

"Hush. Time flees." She took a breath. "I had intended merely to follow you. Until you lured me into the trap and had the misfortune to be arrested." She stopped, puzzled. "How was it you guessed you had been followed aboard the ship?"

"The manner in which three hardened sailors fell at the wave of my sword. It was the same mysterious manner in which my soldiers fell at Magnus."

Katherine giggled. "The surprise on your face as they fell!" Then she sobered. "A Druid trick. Which we are happy to use when it benefits us. Short, thick hollow straws. A puff of breath directs a tiny pellet coated with a sleeping potion. I was in the shadows nearby, watching because I had heard the crewmen speak and knew you were in danger."

A Druid trick. Either she tells the truth and is an Immortal who knows much about the enemy. Or she is the enemy. How do I decide?

Thomas nodded to conceal his doubt. There was yet the major flaw in her words. So he spoke the question aloud. "Why reveal what you did last night? Why now if not ever before?"

"I will tell you now. And there is no need to threaten to throw me overboard," Katherine replied. "When you were arrested, desperate measures were needed. I had to help you and could only do so by playing the role I did. As a noblewoman. And by then, I had also decided you were not a Druid. Not if you were truly going to the Holy Land by yourself."

She hesitates. What does she hide?

Katherine must have caught the doubt in his eyes. "Hawkwood is gone. If you are an Immortal, I need your help as badly as you need mine. It was a risk worth taking. If you are a Druid...I knew I was safe, protected by your gold as a noblewoman there in Lisbon and here on the ship."

Perhaps. But there must be more. It is obvious in her manner.

Thomas thrust his hands through the gap between the iron bars.

She took his hands in hers. Although he had meant the gesture as an appearance of trust, the touch of her hands in his filled him with warmth.

Do not trust her, nor your heart. Yet remember the first time you met her, and how there had been an instinctive reaching of your heart for hers, as if it were remembering a love deeply buried.

Yet he could not ignore the happiness that swelled his throat.

"I pray in the Holy Land that much more will be revealed to both of us," she said.

A noise from behind startled her into dropping both his hands.

"Thomas," she said quickly, "if it is possible to return safely, I will. Otherwise..."

She picked up the ends of her long cape and disappeared in the opposite direction of an approaching crewman.

Thomas did not see her until the galley reached the harbor of St. Jean d'Acre, the last city of the Crusaders in the Holy Land to fall to the Muslim infidels.

FORTY-TWO

Two crewmen brought Thomas to the deck of the ship as summoned by Katherine. He needed the help given by their rough hands grasping his upper arms to keep him upright. Not only was he weak from the lack of proper food, but the brig had been so cramped his legs were no longer accustomed to bearing his weight. And his ankles were now shackled by chains of iron.

The crewman left him beside Katherine and waited watchfully nearby. Beast whined and wriggled in delight at seeing Thomas.

Katherine, on the other hand, showed no such happiness and remained silent. It would serve neither of them if she appeared anything but the vengeful noblewoman.

Thomas stared past her at the half-ruined towers—still magnificent— rising from the land at the edge of waters of the Mediterranean Sea.

St. Jean d'Acre was a town on a peninsula surrounded entirely by sea. Once—when still in Christian hands—it had been protected by a massive wall that ran across the peninsula, so that the only approach for attack was by water.

The air around him was steamy hot—a heat he had never felt before. The sun seemed much larger than he remembered of the sun in England, and its glare was an attack of fury. The buildings that shimmered before his eyes as the galley grew closer were formed in unfamiliar, sharply rounded curves.

At that moment, despite the heat, Thomas felt a chill replace his anticipation.

This land is so foreign that I am doomed before I begin. Muslims have fought Christians here for centuries, and I step onto their land, not even able to...

Thomas took a deep breath as that new thought almost staggered him.

I have been so intent on reaching the Holy Land I have overlooked the single most obvious barrier to my success here. I do not speak the language!

He wanted badly to discuss this with Katherine, but as he shuffled sideways to whisper his concern, the ship's captain approached.

He was a great bear of a man with swarthy skin and a hooked nose. Curiously, he wore a purple turban.

"M'lady," he said respectfully, "we all wish you Godspeed in the search for your relatives. Many were lost to fine families during the Crusades, and perhaps you will find one or two still alive among the infidels."

He paused, searching for a delicate way to impart advice. "This is a strange land with strange customs. Men...men take insult if a woman shows her face. To be sure, you will have no difficulty finding a buyer for your wool. Yet you must wear this during all times in public, including the times you negotiate with merchants."

The ship's captain held out a black veil.

Katherine slipped it over her head. It stopped short of the clasp at her neck that held her cloak together.

"You have my gratitude," Katherine told the ship's captain. "Would that all I meet might have the grace and kindness that you have extended me."

He bowed slightly, then frowned at Thomas. "Shall we whip him once to ensure meekness ashore?"

Katherine removed the veil, held it in her left hand, and touched her chin with the tip of her right forefinger as she studied Thomas. A mischievous glint escaped her eyes.

"No," she said finally. "I think the shackles should suffice."

⚜

Thomas, unshackled now that they were clear of the galley, could hardly believe his ears.

He stood with Katherine in the crowded *fonduk,* a large open-square warehouse on the eastern waterfront. It had belonged to the Venetians before Acre fell to the Muslims. Now, as the best trading area in a town where major trading routes met the sea, it was occupied by hundreds of sharp-eyed Arab merchants.

He stood amazed for one simple reason. The clamoring babble that surrounded him made sense.

"Don't trust his olive oil!" one shout reached him clearly. "That merchant is a crooked as a snake's path!"

"Here for the finest salt!" another voice called out.

"Silk from the overland journeys!"

"Camels for hire!"

Each fragment of excited conversation filtered through his mind.

He understood each word!

And Katherine stood in front of him, her face hidden modestly by her veil, bartering over the price of wool with an eager merchant.

In their language! Impossible…

He stood and watched the chaos around him with an open mouth. The harbor area of Lisbon now seemed like a sleepy town. Beast, too, must have been overwhelmed. He stayed almost beneath his feet, every step, occasionally causing Thomas to stumble.

In all directions were camels, donkeys, and gesturing men in turbans and what looked like long white sheets. There were strange animals with long slender tails—could these be the monkeys of which he had read?—and finely woven carpets, baskets as tall as a man, beggars...

Katherine tugged on his arm.

"I have finished," she said in English. Satisfaction filled her words. "As predicted, I have doubled my investment."

"*Our* investment." Thomas felt the need to immediately correct her, although more pressing things engaged him.

He leaned forward.

"Their words!" he said. "I understand them."

"As well you should," Katherine replied. "It is—"

A beggar darted up to her and chattered excitedly. "Lady, lady, from where did you get such a fine clasp?"

Katherine reached for her neck and touched it in response.

"I—"

"Very fine! Very fine!" the beggar interrupted. "I can find someone to give you an excellent price for it!"

"I am flattered, of course, yet—"

"Double what you had expected!" the beggar insisted. Then he stopped and looked at her coyly. "Or is it a family heirloom?"

Katherine nodded firmly from behind her veil. "It will never be sold."

Unexpectedly, the beggar darted away without another word.

"Strange," Thomas said. "About this childhood matter..."

"Of course," Katherine reassured him. "But first, we must purchase you clothing that lets you blend among these people. And a sword."

She giggled. "And once again, you are in dire need of time in a public bathhouse."

FORTY-THREE

T wenty-two years had passed since the last banner of any of the German, English, or French Crusader knights had flown at the edge of the Holy Land above the stone walls of the town of St. Jean d'Acre, twenty-two years since shadows of those banners had danced upon the waters of the Mediterranean below.

The town then had been a riot of colors. Merchants from eleven European countries had competed for sales from their great fonduks, all supplied from ships arriving from the sea on one side and from camel caravans led by sharp-eyed Arab traders arriving by the Damascus road on the other.

Yet after nearly two hundred years as the main port to the Holy Land, St. Jean d'Acre, the last of the Crusader strongholds in all of the Holy Land, had finally fallen to Muslim infidels. Jerusalem had fallen long before, then Nazareth—the city of Christ's boyhood—then the fortresses along the Sea of Galilee, and one by one, all the mighty castles of the Crusader knights who had battled and held the land for generations.

St. Jean d'Acre had fallen and now was a mere shell of the trading town it had been. To be sure, merchants still haggled, for occasional ships still arrived. But the walls of the city and the high turrets of its remaining buildings, a glorious illusion of strength from a distance away on the water, were actually war-ravaged and doomed to crumble to dust with age.

Few now were those in the town with fair skin and blue eyes, the sure signs of northern European heritage. And none were those who dared display the colors of any knighthood among the Muslim infidels who so thoroughly dominated the entire land that Jesus Christ Himself had walked during His brief and significant life on earth thirteen hundred years earlier. It seemed prudent, then, to be dressed in a way to disguise the fair skin and light eyes.

"I no longer feel half-dead." Thomas grinned beneath his turban. "A rest tonight in a bed that does not shift with the waves, some food, and I will be ready to conquer the world."

Katherine smiled back.

They gazed at each other in silence for several seconds, forming an island of privacy in the hectic motion of the market around them outside the bathhouse.

Don't let those eyes fool you, Thomas told himself. *Remember, you will only remain with her until you discover the truths you need. There is nothing more to this situation.*

To cover the flush he felt beneath her gaze, Thomas bantered and gestured at his robe and turban and sword at his side. "Do I not appear the perfect infidel? Especially after you tell me how it is I understand their language."

"Perfect," Katherine agreed lightly. "We—"

She frowned.

"Thomas, to your left. Is it not the same beggar who approached me about this clasp?"

Thomas turned his head quickly enough to see the beggar grasping the sleeve of two large men and pointing in their direction.

"The same," Thomas confirmed.

All eyes locked across the space between them. The beggar and his companions were each armed with scimitars, those great curving swords. And Thomas and Katherine staring back at them in return.

"Do you find a startling resemblance between those two men and a pair of wolves?" Thomas asked softly without removing his eyes from them.

"Hungry wolves," Katherine said. "I like this not. We should return to the inn and see to your puppy immediately."

They backed away quickly. And soon discovered they were indeed prey for the two large men.

In a half run, Katherine and Thomas darted around market stalls and through crowds of people.

"This way!" Katherine cried.

"No..." But Thomas did not protest in time. Katherine had already chosen a narrow alley.

Why have they chosen us? Thomas wondered as he ran. *Because we are foreign? Surely it cannot be because of the Druids. We have only just arrived.*

Thomas nearly stumbled on the uneven stone of the streets as he stopped and turned to run after her. His sword slapped against his side.

I pray I will not need to use this weapon, he thought. *These men are larger and stronger.*

The two men gained ground. They were familiar with the twists of the alley. Thomas and Katherine were not.

Each second brought the men closer and closer. Thomas and Katherine were now in a full run, slipping beneath archways and around blind corners.

"Again! This way!" Katherine panted. "We are nearly there!"

"No...," Thomas moaned. He did not know the town at all, but knew with certainty her path led them away both from the waterfront and from the inn.

Without warning, Katherine stopped and pounded on a door hidden in a recess in the alley.

"That is not the inn!" Thomas warned.

"Behind you!" Katherine said. She banged the door with her fist, while staring in horror at the approaching swordsmen.

Thomas did the only thing he could. He drew his sword.

Katherine pounded on the door.

"You cannot avoid the assassins' pledge," the first man snarled as he lifted his scimitar.

Thomas managed to parry the first blow, then step aside as the other swung.

I have only seconds to live, he realized. *In cramped quarters, against those great swords, I might as well be dead.*

"Katherine," he said quickly. "Run while you might."

In answer, he felt her presence plucked from his side.

The door has opened, he realized with the part of his mind that was not focused on survival.

Another whistling blow. Thomas met it with his own steel, and the echoing *clank* was almost as painful as the jar of contact that shivered up his arm.

Thomas brandished his sword and prepared for a counterattack.

If I'm to die, they will pay the price.

Both men hesitated and stepped back.

"Cowards!" Thomas cried in the full heat of battle.

"No," came a strangely familiar voice from the very spot Katherine had stood only moments earlier. "They are simply prudent."

Both men stepped back farther.

"Yes," the voice continued, now directed at them. "This crossbow truly reaches farther and faster than the sword. Go back to the men who hired you. Tell them the blood they wish to spill is now under protection."

The swordsmen nodded and quickly spun around, then hurried around the nearest corner of the alley.

Thomas, still panting, turned to look at his rescuer.

"Well, puppy," he was greeted. "Must we always meet in such troubled circumstances?"

Thomas only stared in return.

Sir William. The knight who helped me conquer Magnus. The knight who disappeared three seasons ago on his own private quest.

Thomas finally found his voice. "You describe harmless gnats such as those two as trouble? Truly, you must be growing old."

Now, as when the knight had bidden farewell long ago in Magnus, Thomas fought a lump in his throat.

Then, an early morning breeze had gently flapped the knight's colors against the stallion beneath him. Behind them both had been the walls of Magnus. Ahead of them had been the winding trail that had taken the knight to a destination he could not reveal.

This destination.

St. Jean D'Acre. On the edge of the Holy Land.

The sorrow Thomas felt in remembering their farewell mixed like a sweet wine with the sorrow of a renewed remembrance of Magnus.

He blinked back emotion.

Sir William smiled, switched the crossbow to his left hand, and extended his right hand in a clasp of greeting.

The knight had changed little. Still darkly tanned, hair still cropped short, now with a trace of gray at the edges. Blue eyes still as deep as they were careful to hide thoughts. And always, that ragged scar down his right cheek.

A sudden thought struck Thomas.

"You are one of us." Although it was a guess, Thomas spoke it as a statement. "An Immortal."

FORTY-FOUR

The assassins had failed. It had been so simple to follow Thomas by learning his destination on each of the ships that had taken him. It should have been equally simple to arrange what she wanted. Their instructions had been to kill the woman and capture Thomas alive. Her plan had been to eliminate the woman and appear to rescue Thomas. That would have been so satisfying. Both aspects: Eliminating Katherine, who had spent far too long with Thomas for Isabelle's liking. And to sweep in and rescue Thomas and earn his trust and his arms around her in gratitude.

But the assassins had failed.

They had returned to Isabelle at the harbor with a description of a knight armed with a crossbow. A knight with a curving scar down his face.

Isabelle well knew this knight. She had traveled with him and Thomas—it seemed like a lifetime earlier—on their quest to conquer Magnus.

It did not surprise her that the knight was in this land too.

After some thought, she realized it was merely a complication.

The three of them were unaware she was here; whatever was ahead, it would be easy enough to ensure that the woman and the knight died together.

Once Thomas was alone, he would belong to her.

See where Thomas's journey began

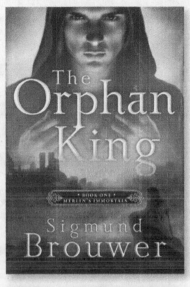

Before Magnus, Thomas was an orphan with a destiny. Catch the beginning of his journey in *The Orphan King,* book 1 of Merlin's Immortals.

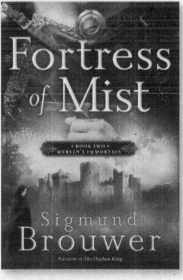

Follow the story of orphan Thomas as he works to retake the kingdom for the Immortals and then is caught between Druids, corrupt noblemen, and unknown enemies. Can secrets from his past conquer the evil he now faces and save his kingdom?